LAUNCH

C.P. HIND

authorHOUSE®

AuthorHouse™
1663 Liberty Drive
Bloomington, IN 47403
www.authorhouse.com
Phone: 1 (800) 839-8640

Published by AuthorHouse 06/14/2019

ISBN: 978-1-5462-4200-0 (sc)
ISBN: 978-1-5462-4201-7 (e)

Main Characters

Harry Stone	Trends Analyst for the Criminal Investigation Service (CIS)
Paul Miles	Chief Analyst of Criminal Trends division. (CIS)
Charles Springfield	Field Agent (CIS)
Susan Stone	Wife of Harry Stone
Rosemary Pearson	Manager Armstrong Mining Facility
Karl Fisher	Armstrong Base Security Officer

PROLOGUE

Earth had undergone a massive reorganisation after the 2025 World Terrorist Conflict. Although no Government officially sanctioned or appeared to be actively involved in this conflict terrorists both religious and economic fought with each other on such a global scale that their actions shattered economies and destabilised political infrastructures worldwide. Oil stocks were at an all-time low, with the result that more reliance was being placed on thermonuclear power. Individual governments of the world threw more and more effort and assets into ending the multifaceted terrorist activities often to the detriment of their own people. Responsibility to maintain basic civil infrastructure including energy supply was gradually subcontracted from government agencies to huge multinational contractors. The multitude of conflicts finally ended after a series of thermonuclear mega power station accidents threatened global survival with an overwhelming radiation fallout affecting two thirds of the globe and threatening the very existence of life itself. A hundred million people perished within one month.

As all of these accidents took place over a matter of two days, there was some debate as to whether they were deliberate acts of sabotage. However, as no one faction claimed responsibility, this theory was discounted. A common design fault was more likely as all of these incidents involved the ten most recently commissioned off-shore mega power plants. These thermonuclear power stations used a new technology designed to produce power at a rate one hundred times the normal output of a standard on-shore power station. As nothing survived the initial detonations it will never be known what really went wrong. There only remained speculation and argument by nuclear engineers that cost saving may have been the root cause.

As part of their basic design all of the new power stations were partially submerged for cooling purposes. Sadly this resulted in eleven countries in the Indian Ocean being deluged by radioactive particles carried by a tsunami. This also occurred on the coastlines of Africa, North America and Europe. South America and the Caribbean nations suffered to a lesser degree as there was only one power station situated within the Caribbean. Despite this the damage to fishing and food production reduced these nations to abject poverty.

A board of inquiry suggested that the companies involved in construction and operation of the power stations had failed to instigate both engineering and personnel failsafe measures and may have been be guilty of not testing the new systems adequately before commissioning. It was also suggested that financial expedience may have been a contributing factor. However nothing definite was proved. Some middle ranking company officers were sacrificed, but these were widely recognised as convenient scapegoats.

All that is certain was that the explosions and resultant radiation fallout from each power station effectively threatened life both in the sea and on land within a radius of approximately three thousand kilometres from each of the ten sites.

It took these catastrophes to bring all the governments of the world to the conference table in Geneva to effect a unified approach to disaster relief. As nearly all nations were affected to a greater or lesser degree a formal World Senate was formed to oversee humanitarian aid programs worldwide. As a precautionary measure all nuclear fission power plants were decommissioned, and a massive worldwide effort was made to substitute them with renewable energy including the development and introduction of nuclear fusion power stations. All races of the planet came together in this titanic endeavour to rescue human and animal species. After some thirty years the world heaved a sigh of relief and survived, sadly at a cost of many species and a much reduced human population. Their deaths were caused by starvation and disease resulting from poverty. Some four hundred million people perished in total mostly in the developing countries involved in the initial conflict areas, and sixty per cent of the diversity of animal species perished.

Thirty-five years after the disaster the earth had recovered sufficiently to allow Mankind once again to explore its own solar system, this time with the added impetus to look for alternative habitable worlds. This exploration was under the control of the World Senate that had effectively become the world's government, comprising equal numbers of representative senators from each of the surviving countries. No matter how small those countries were they had equal representation. Space exploration was subcontracted to huge multinational companies that were monitored and controlled by the Senate, the biggest of these being Transglobal Earth Mining Corporation (TEMCO). This company, while technically within the private sector, was controlled largely by a board of directors selected from members of the World Senate.

After the collapse of many member nations, one of the Senate's first actions was to re-establish law and order on a global level. It was decreed that A Global Law Enforcement agency was to be established, answerable only to the Senate in Geneva and to be coordinated and controlled by a small neutral country. This agency was to be staffed by agents and senior police chiefs drawn from all member countries with the position of Chief Commissioner being rotated every five years. After some lengthy debate, and indeed heated opposition by the more powerful nations represented in the Senate, Singapore was chosen because of it was one of the few countries that had survived the disaster and had successfully integrated and understood the cultures of the Middle East, the Indies, the Far East, and the Western Nations. Other countries were similarly considered, but both Malaysia and Indonesia had suffered badly after the nuclear accidents. Thus Singapore became the Headquarters of the Criminal Investigation Service (CIS). It had wide ranging powers to investigate and prosecute any criminal activity that could potentially threaten the security of the World Senate or its individual member nations. This service had the power (with a Senate mandate or warrant) to override local and international police agencies and security services.

To offset the world's power shortage, the Senate ordered TEMCO to accelerate research into Nuclear Fusion power. Unfortunately nuclear fusion required a rare element on Earth called Helium -3 or He3. China held most of the stocks of this element and in only very limited supply. The moon however had abundant supplies of He3 sequestered in its soil. TEMCO was directed to build a mining facility on the moon.

CHAPTER 1

ARMSTRONG LUNAR LAUNCH SITE

The Armstrong Launch and Mining Site sat brooding on the dark lunar landscape. Originally constructed in 2050 by the Transglobal Earth Mining Corporation (TEMCO), Armstrong Base was primarily built to support the mining and transportation of liquid Helium-3 for Earth's multitude fusion reactors. It was laid out like a huge starfish with the domestic and administration areas at the centre, and with each arm terminating in functional areas dedicated to power, life support, mining, manufacturing and shuttle operations. The complex had one more vital role. A by-product of mining operations was the manufacture of hydrazine, the propulsion fuel used for interplanetary transport vehicles.

For economic reasons the company had opted to use a linear accelerator to launch its interplanetary payloads. The single launch hover-rail and the accelerator's super-conducting magnetic coils ran for some 30 kilometres up a gradual slope terminating at the top of an adjacent mountain. At this point the shuttle reached its launch velocity of 2.4 kilometres per second, and was propelled into orbit. This system allowed escape velocities to be reached at a much reduced cost per payload. On achieving orbit a moderate boost by an on-board engine propelled the space-craft towards its destination.

A bank of high efficiency solar arrays covering some five square kilometres provided the main source of power for the Base and for mining operations, supplemented by an extensive high power battery bank and a thermonuclear reactor needed during lunar dark phases. The latter was the only remaining reactor after the Great 2025 incident, when all such power plants on Earth were decommissioned and replaced by fusion reactors and renewable energy systems.

Shortly after its construction Armstrong Base was sequestered by the World Senate as a launch facility for government sponsored interplanetary travel, specifically to Mars and the moons of Jupiter. The Moon's near vacuum and low gravity allowed the linear accelerator to launch Earth and Interplanetary vehicles, carrying heavy payloads, deep into space with minimal fuel expenditure. Under the control of a foolproof multi-redundant safety system countless launches had taken place over the intervening years.…

SABOTAGE

The man moved furtively along the narrow corridor leading to the reactor room door. He knew what he was doing was wrong, but what could he do? He had no choice. He was carrying a very small device no bigger than a packet of chewing gum. The resulting explosion would not be heard more than three metres away, but the heat and cutting power of the explosive was enough for the purpose. He moved silently passed the door and closed it behind him. This part of the Base had been neglected for more than twenty years, and only the Reactor Engineer came here once a week to check the integrity of the containment vessel. Even that was automated and required only a few short minutes to accomplish. The Engineer had done his inspection that morning so the device would not be detected.

Since the *Great Conflict,* Mankind had developed a fear of nuclear fission products and nobody in their right mind would voluntarily come in here and risk exposure to even a small dose of radiation. This fear was completely out of context with reality because space travellers received far higher doses of radiation with no harmful effects. But the taboo was so great that it overrode normal common sense.

He quickly placed the package against a small pipe that led to the containment vessel wall, then hastily moved out of the room, breathing a sigh of relief as he left. The device had a small green light which winked to red as the man left the building.

The explosion tore a hole in the reactor coolant feed, but that was enough to scram the reactor core. Lights flickered as emergency power cut in. The man sighed and went to his work station.

Two days later, after he had completed his shift in the mine, the man returned to his apartment and poured himself a mug of coffee. As he gulped his first mouthful he thought about what he had done two days ago, and shivered at the memory. Had he been seen? The thought was stillborn. His chest suddenly became tight as he struggled to get air into his lungs. Eyes wide with fear, a thought flashed into his mind, 'What's happening to me?' Panic set in as his breathing became convulsive. Summoning all his strength he managed to take a great gulp of air into his lungs. Then without warning he lost control of his bowels and bladder. A look of horror spread across his face as he tried to take a pace forward, but his legs collapsed under him and he fell helplessly onto his face. His eyes dimmed and he could no longer move.

BASE MANAGEMENT OFFICE

The Base Manager, Rosemary Pearson, looked with horror at the screen image then turned away, a tear running down her cheek. After a few moments, she got up and washed her face in the small sink. She paused with the towel to her forehead, then throwing the towel into the corner, moved back to the screen and called Security. The Security Officer's face appeared on the screen. He was a well-built man in his late thirties, prematurely greying.

"Karl Fisher" he said.

"Pearson here, I have a code red on the physiology monitor for Mark Graham, room 23. It appears terminal."

"Nice way to put it Ma'am I'll check it right away. Has Medical been informed?"

"No, it only just recorded. Judging by the readings, it's a little late for medical."

"I'll call them anyway" said Fisher.

"If you must."

"Procedure, Ma'am."

"Listen Fisher, the monitor indicates this to be a simple heart attack, I don't want your bloody elephant trackers stamping all over the place making mountains out of molehills ... Do you understand me!"

"Yes *Ma'am*." Fisher went bright red, as he promised himself that he would nail the bitch for something before he left Armstrong. The screen went blank.

There was no love lost between these two. Ever since the disappearance of Eric Carlsen, the maintenance man, she had been trying to smooth over every abnormal event in order to give the impression of a harmonious working environment. The reality could not be further from the truth as a result, she had alienated her Security staff and her work force alike.

The Manager sat at her desk, covering her face with her hands, her body shaking uncontrollably, tears splashing onto her desk top.

ARMSTRONG BASE ONE MONTH LATER

It was a routine trip, one of the hundreds of regular launches since the system was installed. The pilot, relaxed and content, was returning home to his family after being away for three months. His main cargo was liquid Helium-3 and an additional priority cargo for *Transglobal*. He was not aware of the exact nature of this second cargo, suffice that he knew that its overall mass was 100 kilograms. This mass data was needed for payload calculations. However, none of that was his concern. At this moment getting off the ground was.

The shuttle sat hovering just above the surface of the guide rail, suspended on its super-conducting magnetics. The pilot yawned, having just completed his pre-flight check. Throwing his arms wide and stretching he spoke into his helmet, "Traffic Control, permission to launch?"

His helmet headset crackled into life, "All clear, Mike, you have a launch window of five minutes, have a good flight." The pilot leaned forward, pressed a contact on the console and addressed the launch computer, "Phillip, launch." The computer, keyed to the voice pattern of the pilot, responded "OK Mike, all systems go." The pilot listened with satisfaction to the high pitched whine as the charging accumulators vibrated through the hull. The Shuttle started to move along the rail, gradually picking up speed under the control of its three redundant computers. These computers fired the huge electromagnetic coils in a very precisely timed sequence that pushed the craft forward at a predetermined acceleration rate, each coil firing for a fraction less time than its predecessor to avoid drag. The pilot was pressed hard back into his seat as the shuttle accelerated toward the lift-off point high on the adjacent mountain. The pilot smiled to himself, thinking about his family and their up-coming reunion. The craft was rapidly approaching the launch point, travelling at about 1.9 klm/sec when it happened!

Half way up the mountain slope, the pilot felt a jolt and he was thrown violently forward against the restraining straps as acceleration diminished. The craft seemed to pause and then catch itself again, then continued to accelerate. The events that followed happened in the blink of an eye. Travelling too fast to arrest its forward motion and travelling too slowly to reach escape velocity the shuttle reached the end of the guide rail and became airborne. For a brief moment it appeared to hang in the sky, then pitched nose down as the emergency rockets fired … too late!

The seat restraints parted and the pilot was smashed face first into the console as the shuttle powered into the lunar surface, in a tangle of wreckage and exploding fuel tanks.

CHAPTER 2

ARMSTRONG SHUTTLE LAUNCH BAY

The long tubular form of the Shuttle sat on the guide rail of the linear accelerator, its nose aimed down the 30 kilometre ramp that curved up the side of a nearby mountain range. Beneath the ramp a warm yellow glow streamed onto the stark lunar landscape.

The public address system crackled into life. Harry Stone looked up from his hand computer and gazed unseeingly at the Spartan interior of a passenger lounge half filled with people. Coloured benches contrasted sharply with the dirty white walls of the waiting area. At one end there was an electronic security gate, with a moving ramp leading up a sloping metal corridor to the shuttle loading bay enclosure. Stone had been trying to read, but his mind wouldn't focus. The voice from the speaker was softly feminine and intrusive and brought him out of his reverie. He knew that the voice was not human, just a machine responding to a pre-programmed launch sequence. From now on his destiny would be controlled by this machine. *"Will all passengers move to the departure area and deposit any returnable or excess mass in the chutes provided, thank you... click."*

Pocketing his small computer he rose and made his way through the crowd of people to the boarding gate. 'God, it will be nice to get back home,' he thought. It felt as if he'd been away for years. In fact, only two months had elapsed since that long and tearful farewell with Susan at the Kuala Lumpur launch site. He was weary and his head thumped.

The sterile and precisely controlled atmosphere dried his throat and pulled at his eyes. He shuddered at the thought that he might have to come back here.

Stone was taller than average, with short black hair, with a physique and aura that made him attractive to many women, but rarely did he notice the effect he had on other people. He was Chief Trends Analyst for the Criminal Investigation Service. For two months he had been gathering information on the activities of the recently emerged organisation styling itself the *Lunar Protection Society (LPS)*. Copying some of the methods of the old Green Movement, the LPS had threatened to prevent mining on the Moon. This was followed firstly by a reactor accident and then by the shuttle disaster. Coincidence? However it was not his job to investigate these incidents. That was for a Field Operative. His job was to gather information on personnel employed at the Base, with a view to their involvement in the activities of this Society.

> The original Green Movement had achieved its aims in the previous century, during the most violent era of human history, and had long been an institution with worldwide acceptance. Operating out of its headquarters in Geneva, the Green Office independently monitored Earth's natural resources, and had become an integral part of the World governing body. Funded by the World Senate, it was the ultimate controlling body for exploitation of all natural resources within the Solar System. As a result of its efforts, most high polluting industries now operated from the Moon or from vast orbiting factories. Power on the Earth was derived by either renewable energy sources or fusion reactors.

'Hell, it would have been worse living on earth in the early twenties than living here,' he thought. Moving to the exit tube, he pondered what it would have been like to breath air that contained large quantities of hydrocarbon waste. Finding this hard to imagine, he shook his head to clear his thoughts and concentrated on the procedure for boarding the Shuttle.

After passing his ID through the electronic gate teller, he stepped onto the conveyer that moved him silently onto the embarkation platform. He noticed several attendants directing people into the passenger bay, but they ignored him as he appeared. He shrugged with indifference, he had been an outsider for his whole stay at Armstrong ... nobody had wanted to know him.

He stood waiting for several minutes, and was just about to say something, when a small pale-skinned attendant tapped him on the shoulder.

"Going home so soon?" Stone recognised the man as a company employee.

"Not soon enough for me," replied Stone. He let himself be led into the cramped confines of the shuttle's passenger cabin and settled himself into a reclined acceleration couch, feeling as always, the sense of helplessness that he got when his destiny was under the control of others.

From now on his very existence would depend upon an unseen pilot and a myriad of electronic devices that would all have to work perfectly in unison for a successful launch. He shuddered. Looking around he noticed the other passengers who all appeared preoccupied with their own thoughts ... staring at the upper bulkhead ... nervously adjusting their couch webbing or twisting their fingers together ... but all maintaining a stoic expression.

"As if it would make any difference," he muttered, panic momentarily rising in him. Rubbing his face with his open hands he settled back and tried to relax. This reaction was most unusual for him, normally he was a very calm and methodical man. Dismissing the thought, he put it down to the previous shuttle accident preying on his mind. The attendant bent over him and adjusted his webbing.

"You look terrible, mate." As pulled the straps tight he added, "I shouldn't worry, it's been four months since we lost a shuttle, and that was only cargo. Mind you, the Company was real pissed, lost billions they did." Then Stone remembered, he had sat next to this man at the company canteen several hours ago. It was strange, he had felt no need to seek the company of others during his stay at *Armstrong,* but now as he was leaving he wished he had made more of an effort to be sociable.

"How long have you been here?" he inquired, using conversation to mask his fear.

"Five years last month by my reckoning" replied the attendant.

"Don't you miss Earth?"

"Not much point is there matey. Besides, I can't go home now, all my muscles have gone soft, I'd be dead inside a few weeks." He looked thoughtful as he spoke, then smiled again.

"Don't miss anything though, came here to get away from the law, and I'm still here. Got my own home and family, all that I need really."

> The attendant was referring to the Criminal Amnesty Act that applied to people who had committed certain non-violent but serious crimes and who volunteered for long-term lunar employment.

As he spoke, a quiet chime sounded throughout the cabin.

"Got to be going, best of luck mate," he said, heading with practiced ease towards the hatchway. Turning, he looked back and waved, "Give my regards to Earth!" Then he was gone; the hatch sighing closed behind him.

The whine of the charging solid state accumulators vibrated through the decking, rising in pitch until it was just on the verge of human hearing, more of a pressure on his ear drums than a sound. It set Stone's teeth on edge, his jaw was aching with tension, the panic rising in him, matching the rise in pitch.

A soft feminine voice echoed from above him,

"Ladies and gentlemen, welcome to shuttle flight LS 73 ... Acceleration will commence in 30 seconds, please relax and have a nice flight... click.".

The pressure came on him, gently at first, as the magnetic fields took hold of the craft, each magnetic coil firing in sequence, gradually increasing in strength until he was pressed deep into the resilient couch.

It seemed to go on forever, his eyes hurt and he had difficulty breathing. Then, suddenly, without warning the pressure was gone, leaving him tingling from head to foot. The accelerator's giant magnets having done their job now rested, silently waiting for their next task.

After a short while, the attitude thrusters aboard the shuttle hissed and whined, then several minutes later, he could feel the main motor fire, pressing him gently into his seat once more, then all went silent. He was weightless.

Stone opened his eyes and looked about him and relaxed, everything was as it should be and he was on his way home. He noticed the other passengers looking at each other smiling with relief. Quiet music piped over the cabin speakers.

Looking for something to do, to while away the trip, he took out his pocket computer. 'I may as well use the time to do a final check before I write my report.' he thought. He spoke into the machine.

"Matthew! Correlate probabilities from Armstrong file."

No trends greater that 30% for criminal intent said the tiny voice echoing from the bone conducting speakers embedded behind his ears. These embedded devices allowed him to communicate with his personal phone and his hand computer. The data didn't make sense, but then humans have a way of corrupting the most carefully designed 'Guess' system.

The little screen displayed several possible scenarios:

Scenario	%	Further Action
1. Prior warning of arrival	29	Security leak … Notify Internal Affairs
2. Deep sleepers involved	20	In depth personnel profiles last 30 years
3. Negative threat scenario	51	Review original data and self-test question list
Summary		
Evidence exists borderline critical 30% for covert activity < 10% for criminal intent.		

The first line on the screen indicated there may have been a warning about his arrival and suggested that any person of interest to him may have gone to ground. Also there was a low probability of a security breach in the Service. The second line displayed a low probability for the existence of long term agents, but suggesting an in-depth search of security profiles. The third suggested the Ottawa Office was knee-jerking at shadows and there was no criminal conspiracy. The latter seemed the most likely. What Stone couldn't understand was the reasoning behind the threat in the first place. No ecological damage was evident, indeed the Green Office had sanctioned the Lunar enterprise nearly twenty five years ago, and no subsequent evidence had surfaced to change that original sanction. What does the LPS want? As far as he knew, the Service had not managed to penetrate any known branches of the movement. They were an enigma, an unknown quantity, it was as if they did not exist. Still, he'd done his job well, cross referencing all responses for two months of interviews and investigations, and still he had come up with nothing tangible!

Either these people were very clever, or the machine was malfunctioning. The latter was not likely and the former even more improbable. Where to go from here!

He addressed the machine again. "Matthew, review last six interviews!" The computer screen went blank.

While he waited Stone thought about his last interview with the Base Manager at Armstrong. Rosemary Pearson was a grey haired career woman of severe appearance. She had not liked being summoned to the office temporally assigned to him. She started the interview by insisting that she was a company executive and would therefore be obliged if the interview could be conducted in her office. Stone knew that the *Guess Sheet Questionnaire* required that all familiar surroundings be removed before the interview commenced. He apologised for the inconvenience and started the questions:

"Give your name for the record if you please."
"Rosemary Jane Pearson" came the chilly reply.
"Your current address on Earth?"

"117 Court road, London."

"Are you married?"

"No!" she paused and looked angry, "What has all this to do with Armstrong's problems?"

"Just answer the questions… How long have you been at Armstrong?"

"Two years"

"Are you affiliated with any known radical organisations?"

There was a slight pause "No"

The questions went on for about two hours, similar questions but phrased in different forms. At the end of the interview the Manager had stormed out of his office. Her responses had stirred Stones interest. After she had left, Stone had requested a summary from his pocket computer.

"Matthew, summarise last interview!" The machine answered in a deep Southern drawl:

The subject seemed nervous and several responses were obvious fabrications..... You may have noticed that there were eleven pauses greater than her average of one second... and her pulse rate and breathing altered significantly indicating either poor memory or unwillingness to provide the truth... The subject's psych file shows no memory problems. Summary: The subject is hiding something with a probability of 89%. Further intuitive questioning is required... Note particularly the three second delay with respect to the current address of her family.

"Matthew! Compile and print all questions with an abnormal time delay or stress index."

A thin stream of plastic emerged from the bottom of the machine. Stone tore off the strip and examined it. Just as he was thinking about the second interview with the Site Manager, the chimes sounded in the Shuttle, bringing him back to the present.

Good time, ladies and gentlemen...this is your captain Pauline Hicks … the shuttle is on target for docking with Gamma 5 in eighteen hours … food is available from the dispenser at the front of the passenger bay … be aware of the weightless conditions and consume food only in the areas designated … Ensure that all eating booth seals are securely closed before commencing your meal … Your toilet needs are at the rear of the cabin if you require to use this facility. Please comply exactly with the instructions affixed to the wall ... Thank you.

Stone was tired and not at all hungry, his eyes drooped closed. 'Time enough time enough for everything' and he dreamt of Susan and his son.

As he slept the little computer continued to work, punching out a long stream of tape, then the screen went blank.

A hand reached over and picked up the small computer and removed the tape. After replacing the machine onto his lap, the hand pressed a small instrument to Stone's bare arm, he stirred in his sleep, but did not waken.

She was small, very slim and about forty going on eighteen, the look of a professional Astronaut. No spring chicken this one, but beautiful in a goddess sort of way. Perfect skin tone and crystal clear blue eyes, contrasting sharply with her short close-cropped blond hair. She was shaking him awake,

"Mr. Stone ... Mr. Stone... wake up!" Her voice commanded attention. He snapped awake.

"Yes, mm." He rubbed his eyes.

"Mr. Stone, please accompany me to the flight deck, sir! ..." Again the command was unmistakable.

"What now, yes of course, thank you." He muttered despondently. He undid his harness and moving too quickly, he started to float upward but she caught him with ease.

"Steady, Sir," she said, "hold on to my belt." He caught her waist belt with his right hand and found himself drifting through the cabin like a great ocean liner in tow behind a minnow tug. They entered the flight deck through a ceiling panel, (if indeed it was the ceiling), it was all so very confusing. He released his grip as she steadied him into a seat next to what must be the pilot's couch.

"There's a coded link with Earth, grab that headset," she said. "I'll be in the galley."

After she left, he donned the headset with some difficulty in the confined space. "Harry, is that you?" said a disembodied voice.

"Who is this?" said Stone

Voice print confirmed ...., Harry Stone ... - 4769 code 99667a ... criminal trends section ... Chief analyst.....

"Bloody hell, Doris! Just a simple *confirmed* will do," said the voice.

Uncoded response, full identification required for transmission to continue, have a nice day.

"God I hate machines!"

"Oh, hello Paul," said Stone with a chuckle. It was a standing section joke that Paul Miles had difficulty using a vending machine, despite being the best programmer/diagnostician in the service. He had a natural talent for seeing the obvious in a welter of confusion and making enormous intuitive leaps from the very slimmest of evidence without the need of a computer. Paul was a recluse, there had to be a good reason for him to call.

"Harry, listen carefully, you're in trouble. You mustn't return to Earth, lay over on Gamma 5 for a day or so and wait for my next call. Do you hear me Harry, don't return!"

That's strange, thought Stone, most unlike Paul. A more steady and unemotional man he'd yet to meet, yet there was a definite edge to the voice, almost panic.

"Paul ... I don't understand, what's the prob ..."

"Harry, look for Springfield..." The voice cut off.

At first he thought it was static, then it dawned on him he was listening to a high pitched squeal, almost animal in its intensity, then silence. He tore off the headset, listening with one ear.

"Paul, Paul? ..." But nothing but a scratching sound ... then *"Unintended break in transmission,"* said Doris with disinterest.

What the bloody hell was going on? His mind was spinning he could not think straight - he was an analyst not a bloody field operative. He must have been sitting for some time, bile rising in his throat, he couldn't move. The next thing he was aware of was the pilot's face, as she stood over him, looking concerned.

"Trouble?" she said.

Stone seemed to be swimming in a sea of confusion, filled with dials and lights, nothing appeared to be where it should be. The pilot's face was moving in and out of focus. He wanted to scream, his mouth opening and closing of its own will. Suddenly he felt very tired and everything went blank. He dreamt he was in a tunnel, going very fast towards a shadowy figure … he could see the face...he could recognise the face, but could not put a name to it, he struggled with himself … then everything blurred.

He awoke feeling light-headed with a sour taste in his mouth, but strangely relaxed. He was still strapped in the couch on the flight deck. In front of him was the deceptively small and uncomplicated control system for the shuttle. Above the control console was a large viewing window. Filling the window was the immense structure of the 'High Orbit Transfer Station,' Gamma 5. He looked to his left and noticed the pilot sitting next to him. She was concentrating on her pocket computer and did not notice him waken.

"Where are we?"

The pilot turned her head. "Oh you're awake, thought we'd lost you … you've been out to it for hours."

He rubbed his face, "What happened?"

"Don't rightly know, Sugar, at a guess I'd say you suffered some kind of shock, that plus Weightless Disorientation Syndrome, must have flipped you over the edge." She made some adjustments to the console. "I gave you a shot of 'SOMIN' to relax you, you were as tight as a drum."

Again he asked, "Where are we?"

The pilot looked around and gave him a very direct stare.

"Just pulling into Gamma 5 docking bay, I just sit here and watch most of the time. Dianne handles the difficult stuff." she said, waving her hand in the general direction of the console. She turned further in her seat,

"Now then Sugar, don't you think you owe me some kind of explanation? I don't usually have passengers go catatonic on me." She looked at him with a mixture of concern and curiosity.

While she had been talking, Stone's mind had been racing back to the message he had received from Paul Miles and the warning that it contained. He came out of his reverie just in time to hear the last bit of the pilot's conversation.

Catatonic shock, rubbish! - he had always been a cool calculating sort of person!

"Did you say I went catatonic?"

"I'm no expert but I've seen space catatonia before, and that's sure what it looked like to me."

He thought about what she had said, he needed someone he could trust to talk things out with ... he was lost in a strange situation and he was alone. He suddenly had an overwhelming desire to share his problems with someone.

"What security rating do you have, Captain?"

She smiled, "All company interplanetary pilots get MAXIMUM -1, near as damn to UNLIMITED as you can get."

She passed over her ID card. He pressed it against the surface of his hand-computer and the reading confirmed what she said. She looked at him as he digested the information and returned her card.

"What I'm about to tell you may *be* UNLIMITED, so be prepared to undergo a high security debrief if anything happens to me." He felt stupid and melodramatic, and wondered why he was talking to the pilot at all. The desire to share was urgent within him.

She looked at him for a moment. "If it's that damned troublesome, Sugar, you'd better keep it to yourself." She started to turn away, he caught her sleeve. "Look, I don't quite know where to start, I need help, listen ... I'm a Trends Analyst with the Criminal Investigation Service. Basically that means I try to plot criminal trends in advance of events, using little bits of information from which I try to piece together the possible future operations of criminal elements on a broad scale. Then I narrow that scale down by intuitive questioning." The pilot looked at him with renewed interest.

"In other words you're a professional snoop," she said.

"In a way... yes... I try to pinpoint trouble before it happens, and sometimes that requires me to ask a series of computer generated questions to activate certain calculable responses. From these responses the interpreter that we call the *Guess Programme* provides a set of scenarios with percentage probabilities. The Service then monitors events and takes action where necessary." He leaned back in his seat to get more comfortable. "About two months ago I was assigned to investigate some problems that had arisen at Armstrong Base. There had been a set of threatening communications from an organisation calling themselves The Lunar Protection Society, a group hitherto unknown to the Service. About five months ago they threatened to destroy all installations left on the Moon, beginning one month after the initial warning."

The Pilot held up her hand and momentarily concentrated on the control board, then turned to look at him again.

"Since then there has been a reactor accident, albeit causing minor damage. And you will be aware that a shuttle has crashed for no apparent reason."

Stone was sweating profusely, he wiped his brow. "Go on," said the Captain.

"Well, I arrived at 'Armstrong' two months ago to action some *GUESS* questions and make an attempt at extrapolation." He paused for a moment, thinking back over some of the interviews he had conducted, he shook his head. "As far as I know there are no correlations or abnormal responses to activate a 'Guess' greater than thirty percent probability, in my world ... that means a big fat zero."

"So what was the call all about?"

He was surprised by the question and a thought crossed his mind, 'Is she being curious or is it something else? Paranoia, - no, something was definitely wrong, he was not usually this talkative.' he made a decision.

"A routine security check, instructing me to continue my investigations at Gamma 5."

She looked disappointed.

"That doesn't account for your reaction, does it? Still, it's none of my business." She turned back to the console.

He felt strangely guilty about having deceived her. 'Now that's a peculiar reaction for an investigator,' he thought.

The Transfer station now filled the front view screen and the docking bay was distinctly visible as a small silver circle surrounded by lights. They sat in silence for an hour while the shuttle inched its way forward and the circle grew larger until it disappeared under the front of the craft. There was a barely perceptible nudge then a loud clang reverberated through the hull. The Pilot said something into her headset and a prolonged hiss sounded throughout the ship. Stone's ears popped, he swallowed hard and they cleared. The pilot swung around in her seat.

"This is where we part company, I hope things work out for you. If you need me for anything in the next seventy two hours, I'll be staying at the Navigators Lodge, room 114." She looked at him with interest. He smiled to himself. 'Paranoia! She was only 'coming on' to him, it must get pretty lonely in this line of work' he thought. 'He wasn't too unattractive, although at the moment he felt old and tired.'

"Er, yes, thanks, I'll remember that." He stood or tried to, and succeeded only in drifting upward, until she caught him by the ankle and pulled him down toward the decking.

"Careful, sir!" She smiled and gave him a gentle push toward the drop hatch in the floor of the flight deck. "See you around, sometime," she said a little wistfully.

He turned and looked at her,

"I'm sure I would be delighted, however..." He shrugged and turned, then stopped, and turned again. "Thanks for all your help,"

"Not a problem, Sugar, any time."

Feeling awkward, he waved, "So long."

He turned towards the hatch feeling a confusion of emotions, and pushed himself down the opening headfirst until he reached the passenger deck. He righted himself with some difficulty and pulled himself along the seat strapping to the waiting attendant at the main hatchway. The man smiled the automatic smile of a professional hospitality worker,

"Good-times, sir, welcome to Gamma 5."

CHAPTER

3

GAMMA 5

Gamma 5 was a vast cylindrical structure, measuring some 5 kilometres along its central axis and 2.5 kilometres in diameter. Accommodation was provided on three deck levels situated round the outer circumference of the station. The agricultural and industrial pods were situated close to the equatorial region. Internal travel around the station between the various areas and decks was accomplished via elevators that worked both horizontally and vertically to the central axis. The entire satellite was self-contained. Fresh food was produced in agricultural pods and consumables were recycled and re-manufactured in the industrial areas. All waste was conserved and with the exception of water, very little resupply from Earth was necessary. Despite all efforts, water was still the most difficult of all recyclables to store in space. Evaporation, no matter how slight, always took its toll.

The gentle rotation of the structure provided a maximum of 1/8 G at the outer hull of the station and gradually diminished as the central axis was approached. The docking ports were situated on each pole of the central axis.

The immediate impression on entering the reception area was one of luxury. The surfaces were less functional than those at Armstrong Base and the lines and decor much softer. Quiet music was playing over the public address system and everything was much more subdued. Even the air he breathed was sweeter. The main reason for this anomaly was the basic design rules applying to each facility. Gamma 5 was designed to meet the needs of transitory and long term residents as well as acting as a near-Earth transfer station for shuttle traffic. Armstrong base, on the other hand was purely functional, a mining and processing plant with living environment for miners, engineers and transit astronauts. Added to this basic difference in functionality, Gamma 5 was much younger and the technology incorporated in its design was more state-of-the-art. Armstrong was constructed 12 years ago, whereas Gamma 5 was only completed within the last 5 years.

Stone collected his belonging from the reception area and headed towards one of the elevators situated on one wall. Pull-along guide ropes were in place to assist the passengers navigate in 0G conditions. Stone looped his belt clip onto one of the guide lines which terminated at an elevator door. Other passengers were already in the elevator when he arrived and he had to manoeuvre his bag in ahead of him. The door closed and the elevator started a gentle apparent downward movement. As it approached the outer periphery, gravity increased and passengers were deposited gently on what was now the floor. Stone had been unable to orientate himself correctly and landed on his side, much to the amusement of the other travellers. Picking himself up he waited for the door to open.

It took some six minutes before the wall enunciator chimed their arrival and the door opened. Although he had stayed at the Station on his way out, Stone was still amazed by the sight before his eyes. He was entering a reception area similar to those of a Five Star hotel on Earth.

Following the stream of passengers, he approached the check-in desk. The male desk clerk was of Asiatic extraction, though it was harder to tell these days with all the interracial mixing that had occurred after the Great Conflicts of 2025. He was extremely well groomed and wore a perfectly tailored one piece flight suit. Stone placed his bag beside the counter and turned to the desk clerk, "I am looking for accommodation for a few days," said Stone.

The clerk looked Stone up and down, judging his financial status with a practiced eye, "Would sir like First Class, or Travel?" Stone was entitled by his position to First Class, but always felt uncomfortable in luxury surroundings, feeling much more relaxed in an environment where he could feel justified in indulging his slightly untidy nature. "Travel, please."

The clerk looked disappointed, but decided to attempt to increase his commission a little.

"Very good sir, may I suggest that one of our Travel Star Rooms with an excellent view of polar Earth and the star field, at only a slightly increased cost."

Stone smiled to himself recognising the manoeuvre, 'this jerk is trying to make a buck out of me, well why not.' "That will do fine."

"Room 1006 sir. That will be 100 credits a day, plus service charge of course" said the clerk handing Stone a card key. "Of course!" said Stone.

He picked up his baggage and headed for the elevator marked 800 - 1060. Entering the elevator he wiped the card against the reader and the door closed. After a slight pause the elevator moved in an apparent upward direction and halted after some seconds, then there was a sideways lurch as it moved laterally to the circumference of the station. After about two minutes, the chime sounded and the elevator door opened. He was quite surprised to find himself in a well-furnished mini apartment consisting of two rooms and a bathroom cubicle. There was the standard crystal video wall, and a huge view window looking down at the African continent that drifted slightly downwards as he watched, but there was a noticeable absence of a star field.

'I'll bet my life that this isn't Star Travel class, I've been had,' he smiled to himself. '*Back to civilisation*, first a shower, then some sleep.'

The shower stall consisted of a 4 foot by 7 foot, glassed-in area. A large extractor fan activated as soon as he entered and sealed the cubicle door, causing his ears to pop. Water immediately began spraying on him from four directions. As the warm water showered over him he noticed that the drain in the floor applied a powerful suction to remove all traces of water as it hit the surface, and the total absence of steam as the overhead extractor salvaged precious water vapour.

A voice chimed into the cubicle

Patrons will please note that showers are restricted to one session per day and a limit of two minutes is placed on each session. Thank you for your attention.

Well, that scotches any idea of long showers, he thought hastily grabbing his towel.

Just as he was about to leave the cubicle, the door enunciator sounded. He hurriedly dried off and donned the gown provided. On the wall-screen was the image of a large heavy-set man in his late forties with close cropped dark hair greying at the edges. A pleasant enough looking individual, but the eyes belied the quiet exterior, they were bright and quick.

"Yes," said Stone.

The man on the screen spoke. "You don't know me, but I think we have a mutual friend in the Service ... Paul Miles?"

Stone was confused, thing were happening a little too quickly for him. Then he remembered, '*Springfield* ...' the person that Paul had mentioned in his transmission.

"Are you Springfield?"

"The very same," said the image. "Don't you think it's time you let me in?" The man gestured off screen. "The elevator will only remain for two minutes."

"Oh yes, of course, Door ...Open!" hoping that the room was smart enough to recognise the voiceprint from his ID card. The door obediently slid open.

The wall screen had not done this man justice; he was massive in all proportions. Not an ounce of fat was visible and he exuded sheer power in every movement as he entered the room.

He smiled, "Aren't you going to offer me a drink, I've been looking everywhere for you and I'm bloody thirsty."

Stone felt a little overawed by this man and stood looking at him for a moment, then suddenly snapped into the present.

"Sorry, I wasn't expecting anyone so soon. Of course, take a seat and I'll see what I can find." The man moved into the room with surprising grace for his size.

"Try the cooler in the other room," the man offered helpfully. Stone made his way into the second room and located the cooler. Removing two beers from the shelf he returned to find his guest looking at his computer, turning it over in his hand.

"Nice model this, had one myself." He flipped it over. "Until it got accidentally crushed in my back pocket when I sat down." He removed a solid steel case from his inside pocket, somewhat larger than the little 'hand held' that Stone used, but similar in its layout.

"Now I use this one," holding it up. "This is Fred. Say hello to Mr. Stone Fred,"

The computer responded immediately, *Good time, Mr Stone ... or can I call you Harry?* chimed the voice in a rich Cockney accent.

"Harry will do fine," answered Stone, a little amused.

"Had him reprogrammed to make him a little more human," explained Springfield, pushing the computer back into his pocket. Taking his beer in his massive hand with the container almost disappearing in its grip, "Cheers!" he said as he drank the entire contents in one swallow. "That's better," he said wiping his mouth. "Now down to business."

Stone felt as if he was on some roller coaster ride, everything was moving too fast for his liking.

"Wait a moment. Before we go any further can I see your identification?"

"Sure," replied Springfield, "not that it will do you much good. On average I get issued with four of these every year, not one the same." Springfield handed over his ID and Stone after retrieving his computer from the bed, wiped the card through the slot at the top. The computer chimed *Springfield Charles ... Company Executive ... The Trans Earth Mining Corporation ... Security unlimited.*

The little machine went silent. Stone digested the information, a civilian with UNLIMITED rating was not common.

"Satisfied?" said Springfield, heading for the cooler and retrieving another beer. He moved across the room and deposited his huge bulk onto the couch, almost filling the two seater.

"It doesn't tell me much," replied Stone leaning across and handing back the card.

"So you're a mining executive. So what?"

The big man took the card back. "They told me you were the best in the business, at least Paul Miles seems to think so."

As he spoke he rolled up his sleeve revealing a faint scar line. Reaching forward, he took Stones computer from him and pressed the screen against the scar. The little computer burst into life *Falstaff Alfred … Inspector … Security Division Criminal Investigation Service … I – 999 Code 7777 Alpha.*

Falstaff handed back the machine. There was a pregnant silence for a few seconds as Stone thought about what the computer had said. In the past he'd had little direct contact with *Field Operatives.* They were the people he ordered to perform unpleasant tasks, but never actually met. They lived in a world of make-believe, totally unlike his quiet, ordered life.

"Well?" said Springfield/Falstaff. Stone's reverie was broken.

"I can only assume that you are working directly for Paul Miles" he said, taking a large drink and feeling the dryness go out of his throat.

"At last you're thinking." Springfield eased himself back in his seat. "Now, if you will sit back and hear what I have to say, then maybe you will be able to help me, and for that matter I, you." Stone got himself another beer and sat next to the bed.

"The organisation known as the Lunar Protection Society or the LPS, have made some serious threats against Transglobal installations at Armstrong. Initially, we received information from Paul Miles at 'TRENDS' suggesting that the threats were just that … threats. We placed a very competent field operative named Eric Carlsen at Armstrong." Springfield got himself another drink and continued. "His initial reports were all negative. Then about four months ago we received a transmission indicating that there was some cause for concern. The reactor at Armstrong appears to have been tampered with, but no official report had been forwarded to Transglobal." He rubbed the back of his neck. "The operative was not too specific because he was suddenly cut off. However, before the transmission ended, he did say that a full report would be sent via the next shuttle." He leaned forward and stared hard at Stone. "That shuttle never arrived, in fact it crashed on take-off, and we haven't heard from our operative since. Now as you are aware Lunar is the only establishment on the three planets that still retains a Fission reactor. The concern that we have is, not so much the reactor itself, although tampering is bad enough, but the fissionable material that remains within it. Earth no longer produces that kind of fissionable material in the quantities that are stored at Armstrong. So we sent another operative at the same time that you were dispatched. That operative could find no trace of Carlsen, nor find any evidence to support his concerns."

Stone couldn't wait. "I was told that there was no absolute evidence of foul play. In fact I've been told nothing about the power plant tampering. As far as I was concerned the reactor incident was an accident, neither was I told that we had lost an operative!" Stone stood up and began pacing.

The big man held up his hand. "Wait, I haven't finished." He continued. "The second operative was told to blend in and make no further communications until instructed. By now, we were rather concerned that we were not just dealing with cranks, but a well organised group." Springfield placed a reassuring hand on Stone's shoulder. "The Investigation Service had not been challenged like this for nearly twenty years. I guess we have gotten a little blasé. Now, this is where you come in. The questionnaire that you took to Luna was not computer generated, but put together by Miles. He has been receiving your reports and analysing them himself."

"So that's why Matthew couldn't make sense of them," broke in Stone.

"That's right ... Miles decided that the information available to the analysers was insufficient to make a decent prediction, an intuitive leap might be what we require. Miles was pretty excited when he called me. He seemed a little nervous and suggested that he might be on to something closer to home than he cared for. He told me that he would redirect you here to help. He knew that if he came himself he would arouse suspicion and decided on the next best thing. He believed that you have the making of a diagnostician and would be able to complete his extrapolation."

Stone looked at the man for a moment. "Is that all? I'm supposed to work out the problem with what you've told me ... Impossible."

The big man looked exasperated. "No, that's not all. Miles was supposed to send a package via the Vancouver Shuttle with all the information he had. The shuttle comes in tomorrow. The only problem is, I can't get hold of Miles to confirm its arrival, or who is carrying it."

Stone looked startled "You don't know, then?"

"Know what?" came the reply.

"Something has happened to Miles. While I was on the shuttle I received a call from him but was cut short, and by the sound of it Miles is either dead or in deep trouble."

He related to Falstaff the details of his return flight including the interlude with the Captain of the shuttle. Falstaff thought for a while. "Roll up your sleeve." Stone was taken aback, "What?" "I said roll up your sleeve" "What for?" "You'll see."

Stone rolled up his sleeve and Falstaff placed a little device on his forearm. The device blinked once and Stone felt a sharp sting.

"Ouch, what was that" he asked. "An analyser," Falstaff answered curtly. "Now hold still."

The little machine clicked a few more times, then a thin sheet rolled out of the top.

"There, that's it," said Falstaff, examining the plasti-paper strip. "When you came around after you fainted did you feel any of the following ... relaxed ... guilty ... talkative?"

"Yes, all of those things."

"Damn ... they are on to us already." He was up on his feet pacing the room. He turned,

"Did you say anything to the Pilot about what Miles told you?"

Stone looked blank. "No, for some reason I decided not to mention that".

"Good, then we are still in business ... What did you say?"

"I told her that I had found nothing and that I was ordered to continue my investigation here."

The big man rubbed his hands together. "Excellent." "Now wait a minute," interjected Stone. "Are you trying to tell me I was drugged on the Shuttle?"

Falstaff looked tired. "Of course you were drugged - unless you are usually that stupid. In which case we're both in trouble." Falstaff rubbed his forehead. "I would guess that you will be back to your normal self in about six hours." He stepped in front of Stone, "As to when you were drugged, I would suggest that it was at least three hours before you boarded the craft, more like four." He took out a tissue and wiped his face with it.

"The analyser indicated you were given a designer drug called Psycotrone, which works at a very low level and undermines the thought processes very slowly. The subject is not aware of any change in his character, and it induces a meek subjective state. All this takes about three hours before the subject is ripe for questioning." He stopped and looked thoughtful. "Incidentally, it was a product developed by the Investigation Service. I've never known it to be in the wrong hands before now."

Stone felt the room moving around him and eased himself into a chair. Falstaff looked concerned and quickly came over to him. Taking out his analyser and making some adjustments he placed it against Stone's arm. There was a whirring noise followed by a click. A stab of pain moved up Stone's arm and tears came into his eyes. He began to sob uncontrollably. The big man held on to his shoulder while his body shook. He tried to grasp reality and the thought came into his head. 'God, I've never felt so miserable in my whole life, totally useless.' The racking sobs continued forever. He didn't remember crawling onto the bed and curling up in a tight foetal position. All the time the gentle giant cooed softly to him. He dreamed of his home in Singapore, of his wife and family, of sitting on a beach under a gently caressing sun, he dreamed ……..

The room was dark when Stone woke up drenched in sweat. "Bloody hell that must have been some beer," he muttered. He lay back on the bed and relaxed. He felt good, the whole world springing into sharp focus. Then he remembered the state he'd been in, the sheer terror of the flight in the shuttle, the message from Paul Miles and the mysterious Falstaff.

He spoke the name, "Falstaff?" The big man entered from the other room.

"Hope you don't mind, I bunked down in the other room." He placed two cups of coffee on the table next to the bed. "I didn't want to leave you in the state you were in."

Stone thought for a moment. "It's all a bit hazy, I can remember feeling confused and lost, but otherwise..." Then he remembered the tearful episode and crying himself to sleep and felt acutely embarrassed. "Look I don't quite know what to say about what happened, but I'm sorry if I caused you any embarrassment."

The big man handed Stone a cup. "Look, mate I've seen some pretty tough characters coming out of Psycotrone neurosis before. Some never recover properly, others go completely hysterical before they normalise. I'd say you're a pretty tough cookie. Besides I accelerated the drug-washing with a pretty powerful stimulant, got you going early, so to speak."

Stone took the steaming hot cup and drank some of the coffee. He looked up over the cup.

"Thanks, Falstaff" the big man nodded,

"That's ok. Just don't call me Falstaff, my name is Springfield, remember? Anyway, call me Charlie." "Thanks Charlie. I'll remember that."

Stone finished his coffee, got out of bed and started to dress. He donned his red flight suit in preference to the grey he had arrived in. 'A mental change,' he thought. "You want breakfast Fals .... Charlie?" The big man grinned, "The smartest thing I've heard you say since I arrived."

Stone pressed the plate marked Room Service and the desk clerk's face appeared on the wall-screen. "This is room 1006, I want two breakfasts with the works now!" Charlie held up three fingers. Stone smiled, "Make that three." The clerk started to smile but Stone cut him off. "By the way, the room is great but it isn't the Star Travel room you promised. I guess you made a mistake. Therefore, rather than complain to the management I will allow you to deduct 20 credits from my bill or find me a Star Suite in a Travel room. Failing that, you can explain yourself to the Fair Trades Council."

The clerk paled, his mouth working but no sound emerging.

Stone continued, "You understand now about breakfast. That will be three for the price of two ...yes?" The clerk shook his head, "Yes ... er ... No ... Yes, sir."

The screen went blank. Stone turned round. Charlie was shaking with silent laughter,

"I've seen it a dozen times, pal, but it still makes me laugh."

Stone looked puzzled, "What does?"

"People coming off the drug nearly always rebound and become aggressively extrovert." Stone looked angry, "Bullshit!" Then caught himself, coloured and smiled. He had enjoyed ragging the clerk, he had actually enjoyed it!

The door chimed, and the head and shoulders of a young woman appeared on the wall, "Room Service!" Stone ordered the door to open and the maid entered. She was in her late teens, and it was obvious from her clumsiness and the fact she wore a *Bahamas University* patch on her right shoulder that she was a student on Compulsory Work Release.

> Since the early Twenty Hundreds it had been discovered that full-time students had found it difficult to integrate into normal life after prolonged study in the closed environment of educational facilities. This led to very highly qualified and indeed very clever people who were absolutely useless at applying their knowledge to everyday living. The World Senate changed this by insisting that before any student could graduate they must *"work their fees"* by providing a service to the State. The type of employment selected was deliberately kept at a menial level, in order that future leaders and pillars of society would be exposed to everyday working conditions. *"Humanising"* was the catchword of the day.

The young girl entered pushing a trolley. There were fresh coffee stains on the cloth covering the top. "I'm sorry about the mess." she fussed about with a cloth trying to dab the stains free. "I only started yesterday and ..."

Stone moved across and took the trolley, "Got your card?" The girl looked startled. "Yes, sir." She handed over her ID. Stone tapped his code into his machine and added 5 credits to her card. She took the card back, then she smiled. "Thank you, sir!" She started to say more but Stone eased her out of the room.

"Make sure that bastard at the desk only sends you up, from now on," he said with a smile.

"Yes, sir." The door slid shut.

Stone rolled the trolley over to the table then moved to the window and looked out. The Earth was slowly creeping across the field of view, bright and blue with the halo of its atmosphere standing clearly away from the globe. He was again looking down on the partly cloud-obscured coastline of the main African Continent but no stars. He suddenly turned to the big man. "Time for business I think, don't you?"

Springfield nodded and took out a notebook, *a real pseudo- paper one*, Stone held out his hand and Springfield passed it over. "I haven't seen one of these for years!" He said, turning the book over in his hand.

"I use it in preference to a machine, I lost a lot of data the last time I broke one of those." He took the book back and held it up. "You can't lose the written word, short of total destruction by fire."

"I still prefer the good old fashioned methods," replied Stone, picking Matthew up from the desk and pressing the activate key. "Good Morning Matthew!" The little machine answered immediately, *Good morning Harry, your voice print is confirmed.* The machine paused How *may I be of assistance?*

"Matthew, respond via speaker and record all human conversations for retrieval from now until cancelled, compress maximum, analyse for deception and human emotion." The computer went silent in his ear and after some seconds the loud speaker reported,

I am now in interview mode. "Thank you, Matthew."

"Springfield, thanks for your help during the last few hours." He picked up a piece of fruit and began chewing on it. "I remember you saying something about a problem that I may be able to help you with, before I passed out last night. How can I help?"

The fruit was unfamiliar to him and was a little tart, he put the remnants in the recycle chute.

Springfield flipped open his note book. "About twenty two hours ago" he began, "I received a priority call from our mutual friend." He started to pace. "During the call he seemed pretty agitated and wanted me to meet you off the shuttle. He said that you had vital information on the activities of the Lunar Protection Society and that I was not to let you out of my sight until he contacted me again." He stopped and looked puzzled. "He then said a very strange thing... he said you probably would not be aware of what you know." He turned to the window and looked out, then look back at Stone. "He said that with a little prompting, plus the information he was sending on the next shuttle, you would probably be able to make an intuitive leap."

Stone shrugged his shoulders, "I don't know what he meant by that ... but go on."

Springfield looked a little sheepish, "He also said that you were an insufferable bore and an arrogant bastard, and unless I insisted you would think that you knew everything and not try to resolve the problem."

Stone flushed, remembering his last meeting with Paul Miles, a small thin man with a receding hairline, fussy by nature and who had made looking untidy into an art form. The man was intolerable, refusing point blank to answer any questions in a straight manner, preferring instead to extract answers by endless counter questions. Although Stones found his habits to be annoying in contrast to his own well-ordered life, he could not help smiling to himself and thinking of the man with some fondness.

"He is probably right, you know. I have noticed some traits in that direction during self-analysis sessions." He stretched and yawned. "However, that's me and I can't change."

Springfield went over to the cooler and took out a beer, the cooler had been automatically refilled during the rest period.

"The nice thing about space, it's always night and you don't feel bad about when you drink." He popped the top, sat down and opened his note book again. "The most obvious question I need to ask you is what did you discover at Luna?"

"Nothing, absolutely nothing." answered Stone, running his hands through his hair. "I was reviewing the data on the shuttle when ...." He stopped and looked at his computer.

"I had just asked Matthew to do an analysis .... I don't remember any results though.

"Matthew, do you have the last analysis I requested?"

The little machine clicked, *Analysis not requested.* The voice sounded strange. *Memory stack overflow ... no data available ... shutting down.* The machine went silent.

Stone rushed over to the table where the machine was sitting and picked it up. "Matthew?" No response. There was no tell-tale light on the front and the crystal screen was blank.

"I've never had a Model 74 malfunction before!"

Springfield took the machine from Stone and pulled his own out of his pocket. He plugged in a communication cord and punched in a code and both machines became active.

Springfield's computer came to life in the comical cockney accent. *The bugger's lost his marbles ... I'm tracking some displaced file location tables. The root cause of the problem is located in the central processor instruction set ... fixing ... He's not as bright as he was, but at least he will work.* Springfield's machine went silent. Springfield unplugged both machines and handed Matthew over to Stone.

"Matthew, status!" The instrument spoke in a monotone all trace of characterisation gone from the voice. *Status Functional ... missing memory block in ....* the machine rattled of a string of memory locations, *Self-repair in progress, this will take approximately twenty four hours to reconstruct file integrity.* Silence.

"This is not possible!" cried Stone. "There's months of work in there."

"Not any more there isn't," said Springfield drily.

CHAPTER 4

S oon after Springfield had left the room, Stone made a cup of coffee and sat down at the hotel terminal. Sipping his coffee he started to think of all the interviews he had conducted on Luna, starting with the plant floor workers. One of the most interesting was one Vladimir Petrovic - a Russian born 2220 in Gorki, both parents deceased, went to Lunar in 2244 as a six month shift worker and stayed on. Stone started to type as he recalled the events. He found they were surprisingly clear in his mind. More surprising was the clarity with which abnormal responses sprang into his mind. He decided to copy only the data that he considered to be significant. The strangest responses involved marriage and relationships. Petrovic had appeared to be uncomfortable answering these questions

"What is your employment?"

"Nuclear power plant engineer."

"Are you contracted in a marriage to any person?"

"No!" The response was almost immediate, far quicker than his average.

"Do you have any obligatory social contracts with another person?"

"I told you NO!" The subject appeared to become very excited.

"Have you lived on Earth for any length of time since your contract with the company?"

"Yes, I took extended leave about two years ago, didn't come back for eighteen months."

"Holiday?"

"Not exactly. I blew my pay in about six months, took a job with World-Wide Mail"

"What made you come back?"

"Money."

The interview continued for another thirty minutes, with no further abnormal responses appearing.

Stone sat back and sipped his coffee. "What's the connection? he muttered. It would not come to him. Out of the five hundred interviews he had conducted, there were only five that were abnormal enough to prompted further investigation. He started to type again. Suddenly a pattern started to emerge. He was stunned, and he sat back looking at his work. It was like a door opening into a completely strange landscape. He knew what he was looking at but it made no sense. He started to go over his notes again.

The door chimed, and Springfield was visible in the viewer. "Door Open!" said Stone.

As the big man entered, Stone swung round in his chair. "Can you get me information on the marital status of these people?" he said, pointing to the computer screen.

"Shouldn't be any problem."

"Good, I think we're onto something."

"What's this got to do with Armstrong Base?"

"Well, all these people have an abnormal response, when questioned about their marital status, or home address. I don't quite understand it just yet, but I think it's relevant."

Springfield pulled out his notebook and made some notes from the screen.

Stone interrupted, "Look at this ... I knew it! See here, the connection is unmistakable!"

Springfield looked and saw nothing but a list of names and loops connecting them.

"I don't quite see what you are getting at."

"Don't you see the connection between all the abnormal responses? ... all but one that is. They are all married long-term Lunar workers who have not transported their wives, i.e., they have all separated from their families."

"Not all," said Springfield.

"No, but this is the first time I have established any sort of correlation." Stone sat back and placed his hands behind his head and looked at the ceiling. "It's a start, Charlie." He suddenly jumped up and headed for the door. "Let's have lunch, then wait and see what comes in with the courier. In the meantime could you check the arrival time of the next shuttle."

GENEVA

"And what has he discovered? ... Nothing!" The old man paced the wood-panelled room. Sitting at a desk was a younger man wearing an expensive grey one-piece suit. The older man continued, "If we overreact now we could spoil everything. The best thing to do leave him where he is. He can't do us any harm from there." The younger man stood up,

"That's all very well for you to say, but you aren't in the hot seat. I am."

The older man crossed the room and stood very close to the desk his face only a few inches from the other. "I said ... do nothing. Got that ... nothing!" He moved back. "If necessary we can eliminate him at any time we choose so leave it be. We don't want to draw any further attention to us or to our objectives." The younger man sat down and mopped his brow. "What about the agent?"

"The agent will do as he is ordered. He isn't a problem," snapped the old man.

"You are sure that no information was passed by Miles?"

"Absolutely. We got to him while he was trying to pass the information, Miles won't be bothering anyone again."

"You didn't kill him?" queried the young man.

"Don't be stupid. Why risk bringing a full scale inquiry down on us. No, he has had a fairly severe nervous breakdown and is being cared for in the best sanatorium in the country." He looked at his fingernails. "A shame, such a wonderful brain. What a waste."

GAMMA 5

The restaurant was situated on the outer skin of the station. The entire wall was a huge window looking out onto the stars with the Earth showing at one edge. Stone was sitting alone looking out at the view as Springfield returned and sat down.

"Your meal arrived while you were away, I hope it's still hot."

"Who cares? I could eat a horse, not that I would eat a protected species...."

Stone spent some moments reading from the table's repeater terminal.

"Now that I think I understand how, all I need know is ... why?"

Springfield was stuffing his mouth from a huge plate of food. He looked up from his task momentarily. "I still don't understand, what's got you excited?"

"You'll have to wait until the courier arrives with the information from Miles but I think I'm getting the picture," said Stone with a smug smile on his face.

Springfield wiped his mouth, "Now then, let's go over what we have. According to you there is a connection between the threat at Armstrong and the family status of four staff members on the Base. I still don't see ... there are about five hundred Base personnel and half of them are married."

Stone held up his hand, "Yes, but only four produced abnormal response reactions to questions relating to their families. They responded normally to all other questions. The only exception was Site Manager, Pearson. She gave four doubtful answers to questions about her family and the situation here regarding the LPS. That in itself is singular."

Springfield called the waiter and ordered a double dessert, then turned back. "Ok, so we have four families, and a hyped up Site Manager who may or may not be mixed up in funny business. So what."

Stone looked at the ceiling, "Don't you see, it has all the hallmarks of a standover situation. I'll bet that you can't trace the families of any of the people on that list. Whereas I'll bet that the Pearson family is intact and that you will find some dirt in her past. Call it a feeling."

Springfield replied, "ok, I'll get Head Office to check on those people, but that still does not tell us what is going on." Stone leaned across the table, "No!"

Springfield was surprised by the vehemence of the response. "Why not?"

"Don't let Head Office know anything just yet. Has it occurred to you that if Miles has gone missing this can only be an inside job?"

Springfield looked alarmed. "You're kidding. There is no possibility that an agent has gone bad, it's never happened in all the time I've been in the Service. The security clearances are far too rigorous, plus the auto destruct implant is a guaranteed way to ensure loyalty. God, you couldn't grow another layer of skin without the bastards knowing about it. Besides, all agents are acoustically monitored unless off planet." He pointed to the slight scar on his arm. "We're all wired."

"Can you get rid of the implant?" asked Stone.

"I could, but I'd be out of a job in seconds and all my credit cards would cease to function, I couldn't operate. Doors wouldn't open to my voice print and a general alert would sound in every cop shop in the solar system." He ran his finger round his collar. "Plus the biological self-destruct would automatically activate within twenty four hours."

"Blast, then you'll just have to work away from me then to give me some space. If they traced you, then they would have me as well."

"What are you saying, Stone? Do you think our bosses are in on this? I can't believe that the IG is involved." Stone considered this answer carefully. "I doubt that the Inspector General is involved, but maybe someone lower in Service or higher, at Senate level is. I really don't know for sure. Call it intuition, if you like. There are a lot of loose threads which are beginning to come together. Do as I say, old man, please."

"Right, no head office." The big man paused in his eating, thought for a moment, then put down his fork and turned the terminal to face him.

"Desk, I want a tight-beam link with Monark Insurance Securities in Ottawa."

The female operator's face appeared on the screen. "That will be 100 credits per minute, sir." "Book it to Transglobal, code TG 18375," said Springfield. The screen went blank for a moment then another female face appeared. "Monark," she said.

"Copy this on scramble," said Springfield holding up his card. "Done!" she responded.

"I need the marital details and family backgrounds on the following people." He held up the notebook to the screen. "Copied!" was the reply.

"Now patch me to Stevens."

"Sir, the Director is very....."

"This is very urgent ... Tell him his big friend wants to talk about a sordid night out in Montreal." Almost immediately the girl's image was replaced by a stocky dark-haired man whose face looked angry. "What the hell?" he said. "Oh, it's you!" The voice became wary. "What do you want?" "Steve, I need your help." said Springfield. "Don't you always." came the reply.

"I've just given your Section a list of names that I want information on. I need the answers to go to me only, no reports to Head Office."

"What are you up to?" Stevens replied, waving his finger.

"Call it an unofficial internal investigation. I don't want anyone to know that I'm chasing these people. Trust me, it's important!"

"Trust you ... you must be joking ... Ok, I'll fix it, but you owe me." The face disappeared for a moment then came back into view. "Anything else?" Springfield thought for a moment.

"Yes, one more thing, Steve. Paul Miles has disappeared, I know you have unusual sources of information. Can you can find him for me, please? I really appreciate your help mate. Delivery to our normal DC place in two days. I'll be waiting at our usual time." Stevens nodded and the screen went blank.

Springfield turned to Stone.

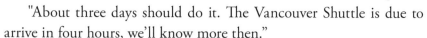

"About three days should do it. The Vancouver Shuttle is due to arrive in four hours, we'll know more then."

The Earth Shuttle Bay was a vast enclosure in the centre of the station. Unlike the Lunar Ferry docking cells, the Earth Shuttle required an enclosed docking maintenance and refuelling area. As soon as the lowering platform had stopped at the unloading point, the two huge doors to space were closed. The sound of rushing air indicated that normal atmospheric conditions were being restored. Soon, maintenance crews were swarming all over the craft and people commenced filing off the ship. It was strange to seen a vessel with wings again, after living in an environment where they were not required. Stone was standing on the viewing platform above the bay floor, looking through the thick aluminium-glass window. He did not quite know what or who he was looking for, but he was sure he would recognise Mile's handiwork, even from where he was standing. Then he saw her as she was just leaving the craft. What the bloody hell she was doing here. Then he recognised the sense of it, Miles could trust no-one else. He hurried to the elevator, entered and hit the ground zero button. This time he remembered to hold onto something.

… It seemed like an eternity since they last slept together. He looked across at his wife's head resting on his shoulder with her right leg across his lower body. He stroked the hair away from her eyes and she stirred and muttered. Their reunion had been like a whirlwind of movement and confusion with endless questions and answers and finally the almost shy reunion in bed. She was tired after her trip but could not sleep until she had satisfied herself that they were together again and convinced herself with a passion that surprised both of them. Then and only then she slept, clinging fiercely to his arm. She was not young, but still maintained that ageless beauty that some Asian women can hold all their life. She had turned thirty eight just before he had left for Luna. She was small-bodied woman of Eurasian appearance, the result of an English father and Chinese mother, black shoulder length hair, a small button nose and cat like blue-green eyes, and a mischievous sense of humour and an acute intelligence that shone through in her nature. Stone saw all these things without seeing them, they had been a part of his life for ten years ever since they had met at a Company seminar in Singapore. He'd been a new addition to the organisation, straight from the academy and she had been a field operative from the Mars division. They had fallen in love almost on meeting, although she had little time to spare between assignments and he was busy learning the ropes in the Trends Division. Their affair was hurried and almost violent in its intensity. They were married six months after their first meeting. Everyone said it would not work, but it did. The cost to her career was great and every now and again Stone would notice a wistful look in her eyes as his career progressed, but she never said anything. Now here she was again, once more working at the job where she had trained so hard to succeed and the life was back in her every movement. It was like stepping back ten years and seeing her as she had been when they first met, alive and full of energy.

He had not asked her about the package and she had not volunteered the fact she was carrying it. They just absorbed each other, not wishing any other influence to interfere with their joy. But now he was anxious to know what Miles had sent him. He fidgeted beside her, willing her to wake up so that he could begin the final analysis. This made him feel guilty, so he refrained from waking her, but he felt frustrated while the problem remained unsolved. Finally he could not stand it any longer. He disentangled himself from her, left the bed and noisily fussed about in the little kitchenette, making coffee.

Carrying two cups he returned to the bed. She was still in the position he had left her in, he sighed loudly. Suddenly she was up and out of bed, the green-white Earthlight shining on her naked body. She jumped across the bed and knocked him to the ground careless of the coffee cups which went flying and kissed him with a passion that soon had them fiercely making love again. After what seemed a long time, with her head resting in the crook of his arm, she looked up and giggled. "I knew you couldn't wait for me to wake, making all that noise in the kitchen. Really Harry!" He looked at her and smiled. "How long have you been awake?"

She pushed him away and sat up. "Oh, about an hour, I just wanted to see how patient you could be." She laughed again. "Not long eh!"

She stood up and reached for the robe that lay on the floor by the shower stall. "Still, I was determined to extract a price." She looked coyly at him. He ignored her and said "Sorry, the fun's over and it's on to business, coffee first?" He got up, picked up the cups where they had fallen and headed for the little kitchen.

"Tell me the story, how did Miles rope you into this?" he said.

"I'd like to say a long story but it wasn't. Miles called me three nights ago and said that he needed me to deliver a package for him to this Station." She headed for the shower stall,

"I wasn't sure at first but your mother said that she didn't mind looking after Michael for a few days and I looked as if I needed a holiday. The next thing I knew, a package was delivered to our Singapore flat. So I did a quick one day refresher at the Centre in KL and here I am." She stepped into the shower and started to wash. "There was something wrong with Miles, though", she said thoughtfully, "I don't think I have ever heard him sound so serious about anything. He was positively edgy."

Stone stood by the shower door, waiting with two more cups of coffee.

"You won't be aware then that Miles is in trouble."

"What?" She said, as her head appeared out of the shower stall, activating the automatic warning about water conservation.

He retold the story about the call from Miles, omitting the details about his drug induced episode more from embarrassment than a desire to protect her from unpleasantness. After all, she had been an operative and was never one to be squeamish.

"Do you think he's dead?" She said, rubbing her hair dry with the towel.

"I don't know, could be." He passed her a coffee cup.

She dropped the towel and took the cup between both her hands and looked at him searchingly. "You're hiding something, out with it." Reluctantly he told her about the Psycotrone episode.

"There's nothing else is there?" she asked, looking over the rim of her cup

"No, that's it. All I need now is the package."

She placed the cup down and started to dress in a green jump-suit. He looked at the form-fitting outfit. She caught his look.... "I don't believe you! Keep your mind on the job, if you please!" She gave him a kiss. "Now, concentrate!"

She reached for her travel pack and rummaged inside it, finally producing what looked like a small flat crystal about one centimetre square. She handed it to him. It was a psych chip. He was stunned. "Who do we know that can use this?" he said, turning the crystal over in his hand. "We need a rigged operative."

> The crystal chip was made of an organic crystalline compound and used for the transmission of very sensitive data. It had to be inserted into a surgically implanted reader a reader which then transmitted the information directly through a cortical link into the sound and vision centres of the brain of the operative who is keyed to relay the information. The beauty is that after a session the operative doesn't remember any details of the transmission and the chip is keyed to only one reader. So that even if it falls into the wrong hands, without the keyed operative the chip is totally useless.

His wife looked at him for some moments, "That will be me."

Stone was stunned. "You? How long have you been rigged?" "Since the second year of my training." She said.

"How come you never told me?" She paused, not wishing to hurt his feelings.

"You never asked and it didn't seem important at the time, and after a while I guess I forgot about it." She saw the strange look in his eyes and crossed to him, holding him close.

"Where is it planted?" He said stiffly. She moved away and lifted her hair, there was a small scar just behind her left ear. He had seen that before but had passed it off as an early school injury. "Does it still work?" She dropped her hair, "Of course."

He couldn't get it out of his mind that his wife was part machine, not a large part, mind you but it disturbed him, which was crazy because the bone conducting microphone and speaker for his own personal phone was embedded behind his ears. The phone itself was worn strapped to his wrist.

"How do you use it?" She produced a small device and inserted the chip. "When you require playback you just place this against the side of my head, and the disk is inserted automatically through the skin, It's quite painless, I assure you"

"And afterwards?" He said. "The chip is bio-degradable and dissolves after four hours, it also contains a healing agent that helps the skin regrow over the reader."

"I think I'm going to need help on this one," he said. "I'll call Springfield." She nodded, "Perhaps that would be best."

A small tear had appeared in the corner of one eye. He saw it and melted. Holding her to him, he thought what an idiot he'd been. "I'm sorry honey, it caught me by surprise."

She nodded and held him closer. They stayed that way for several minutes, finally she disentangled herself from him and wiped her eyes. "Call him now, let's get this over with."

Stone reached for the communicator and dialled Springfield's room. Springfield appeared.

"We need you now." was all that Stone could bring himself to say."

"OK, I'll be there in about ten minutes." the screen went blank.

Stone knew that operatives had many devices implanted during training. Their operational level determined what surgical alterations were made. He was afraid to ask his wife if there were any more surprises in store for him. He realised how little he knew about this woman he had lived with for ten years. Yet somehow it made their relationship even more special. He had never asked before because he knew she would lie to him, security was a terrible thing sometimes.

She moved over to him and placed her hand on his. "If there is anything else you need to know about me, I think I can trust you," she said.

He felt a sudden surge of warmth for this woman. "No, I think

I know all I need." He smiled and kissed her gently on the forehead. Holding hands they moved to the couch and sat, drinking their coffee and quietly enjoying each other's silent company.

The operation to insert the chip took only a few seconds. Stone couldn't watch so he faced the big window as Springfield inserted the device.

"We're ready Harry." Stone turned. Springfield was pressing a pad with a few spots of blood on it to Susan's ear. After a few seconds Springfield moved away. She sat immobile, no expression on her face at all. It was like looking at a marble bust. Suddenly, Miles voice, lifted by one octave sounded through her mouth which moved in perfect unison to the speech. Even the mannerisms reflected that of the speaker, he could almost see Miles in the gestures.

"Hello, Harry. Sorry to do this to you but it is the only way I can be sure that only you and Springfield get this message. First, get Springfield to disable his trace implant. I have adjusted the central computer to ignore his device failure." Springfield left the room.

"There are three categories of responses that I have detected from your transmissions and they involve the family status of six subjects. You may have missed one. However I am confident that you will have detected the others. The second category involves subliminal questions inserted into the interview. You may not have detected any of these, and they involve three of your subjects. I am reasonably certain that these people are actively working for the opposition. The third category involves direct action against the Armstrong Base. Two of your subjects appear to be deeply involved in a conspiracy that constitutes a direct threat to the Base ... I have little time to elaborate, the hounds are closing in on me and I am being constantly watched. The only inference that I have deduced from these data is that the Service is involved in some way and at a very high level. You cannot trust anybody in the Security Services. You will have to act independently in bringing proof of this very real threat. The Inspector General, Walters is the only Executive that you can trust. Bring the evidence home and quickly. I suggest the first place to look for evidence will be on Gamma Five. Then I suggest a return to Armstrong Base. There has to be a link agent who has access to transportation to and from Luna. This goes very deep Harry. Take care."

Stone's wife slumped in her seat, and started to wipe her eyes with the back of her hand. "Bloody hell!" said Springfield from the doorway. He was holding a blood stained cloth, "How do we fight this one?"

Looking at the cloth gave Stone a start, "What about Susan's trace?"

"She doesn't have one, it must have been removed when she left the Organisation. I scanned her before I implanted the chip."

"Then why leave the reader in her head?" said Stone

"Different ball game. That's hooked up to her neural system, too risky to remove without permanently damaging the subject." Springfield looked awkward, "You know about the rest, I assume?" Stone glared at Springfield, then looked at Susan "What rest?"

Springfield shrugged in for a penny, he thought "You've got a very dangerous lady there, you know."

"What are you talking about, Springfield? For god's sake, get to the point!" Stone was getting angrier by the minute.

"She's hot-wired." Said Springfield.

"Hot-wired?" Stone sat down.

"Let me explain. A lot of our ladies and a few male operatives have had their cerebral cortex wired through a small internal protein-based computer. This computer is programmed to initiate a fight or flight response to certain criteria. She can also initiate a response herself independent of the program. The computer then automatically sends a pre-programmed sequence of movements to her limbs. The device is very clever. It can decide the action required to run or fight, overriding the fear process that normally incapacitates people during conflict situations. Additionally, the device provides a much quicker response time than that of normal humans. The higher synaptic voltage triggers the muscles much more quickly and therefore with more power. Sorry, old man she's one mean lady."

Stone couldn't believe his ears.

"You mean to say that at any time during our marriage she could have run amok?"

"That's not what I said, I said she could voluntarily initiate the process. There has never been a single case where a *Speedie* has run amok ... They are specially selected and programmed for stability"

"Speedies, that's what you call them?"

"Yes." Springfield looked away.

Susan had woken during the last part of the conversation. She looked at Stone, with fear in her eyes. Stone paced over to the window, his hands behind his back. He turned suddenly.

"Is that what you were trying to tell me earlier, when you asked if there was anything else I needed to know?" She nodded. "Then I'd better make the coffee and behave myself," he said smiling at her.

She stood and ran to him, "I love you Stone," she said. Springfield took out a tissue and mopped his brow. "This calls for a beer." He rummaged in the fridge and passed two beers over and retrieved one for himself. "I feel much more comfortable now that's all over. Here's to us." He tilted the can back and swallowed.

ARMSTRONG BASE

"Listen, when it comes to general security on this Base, I'm it, not you!" Karl Fisher was in the Manager's office standing over the desk. He was furious. The Manager had just denied him access to the post mortem results on Graham. "And I am the Site Manager ... and have the final say on who has access to information. And I say this information is not relevant for your enquiries." She stood up and faced the Security Chief. "Furthermore, Fisher I also hire and fire on this Base. Any more insubordination from you and you'll find yourself back on Earth with a reference designed to ensure you only work as a toilet cleaner. Do I make myself quite clear?" Fisher backed away from the desk and stood glaring at the Manager. "Quite clear, Ma'am." He turned. "I hope for your sake that what you tell me is correct. If I discover that you have endangered this Base I will submit a report to Earth Central and let them decide who should be removed. Good day, Ma'am," Pearson looked as if she would explode, "Get out!"

Fisher returned to his office and called for his Sergeant Watchman, Bill Gregory. He drew himself a coffee and sat down in front of his console. A few minutes later the Sergeant arrived. He was a smartly dressed professional of about forty years of age and powerfully built. He exuded confidence in his very stance. "You wanted me, Chief?" Fisher stood up and closed the door then turned on the snoop-screen. "Yes, Alan. I've just had an interview with the dragon lady. She won't let me gain access to the post mortem results on Graham ... I think the bitch is hiding something."

The Watch Officer shrugged, "Ok, so what do we do about it?"

"I want her watched. Bug her quarters and keep her under surveillance at all times. Let me know who she speaks to ... and what she has for breakfast, got it?" The Sergeant thought for a moment,

"Bonus share I hope. If this goes wrong we're both in trouble."

Fisher thought for a moment, "Get me something I can use and you'll get triple share, Ok."

Gregory chuckled. "Consider the lady hung." He turned and left the office.

Fisher smiled to himself, Play games with me, will you, we'll see who gets fired, he thought.

GENEVA

It was dark outside the wood-panelled office, where two men were in heated discussion.

"I don't give a damn what I said before. Terminate him!" The younger man threw up his hands.

"I've already told you, we can't trace the operative. Either his trace has malfunctioned or he has removed it!" The older of the two sat heavily behind the ornate desk.

"You told me that was impossible."

"Under normal circumstances it is, but for some reason the computer refuses to perform normal termination procedures and insists that the operative is still transmitting."

"Then manually override the system."

"You can't. There are over one million operatives out there, and the computer for security reasons generates its own codes for each trace."

"So, instruct the machine that the operative is no more."

"We can't do that either. The machine continues to insist that the agent is still active and refuses to close off accounts and facilities. There is only one person in the Service who could pull a stunt like this ...

bloody Miles!" The older man thought for a moment, "Get him and bring him here."

"Are you mad? Miles is in the final stage of cerebral washing. I doubt if he can put on his own shoes at this moment."

"Then stop the treatment, at least until we can discover how he's fixed the system. Besides, who knows what else the bastard may have done!"

The young man turned his wrist over and tapped a code into his personal phone. A white suited figure appeared on the screen,

"Get Miles and bring him to Central." The figure looked puzzled,

"Sir we can't stop treatment, we have almost reached *turn round.*"

"Do it!" the figure disappeared from the screen. The young man turned to his superior. "I hope you know what you are doing."

"So do I'," said the old man. "So do I." He stepped to the window and looked out at the parkland beyond. "I understand that phase two is now complete and we are ready to finish this business."

"Yes, sir. Unfortunately our local man exceeded his orders and terminated the CIS operative, but we have covered that eventuality."

"I see. Leave him be for the moment, there's not much he can do from there. Just block his communications channel to the Company."

"I have already done that, sir."

"Good. Let's have some breakfast while we wait for Miles."

The older man stepped from behind his desk and headed for the door. "Oh, Gordon, no more mistakes, neither of us can afford it. There is a Senate election this year and I need those voting seats, there is too much at stake."

"Yes, Sir."

GAMMA 5

Stone and Susan headed for the Navigators Lounge. "Are you sure that she will still be here, darling?" said Susan.

"No, I'm not sure, but I think so. If my memory serves me, she said she would be stopping over for at least three days."

They entered the Navigators Lounge. The colour scheme was designed to rest the eyes, everything was in subdued pastel blue and green. The atmosphere was almost like that of a library, quiet and genteel. They spotted Hicks sitting at a console, reading. Stone approached and sat down next to her. She looked up. "Well hello there, Honey." She said, turning in her seat. "So you decided to pay me a visit after all."

Stone looked over to his wife, "Not exactly ... I need a favour, Pauline."

"The story of my life, Sugar. What can I do for you?" She placed her hand on Stones knee. "Stone shifted a little, aware of his wife's glare.

"Er, when does your shuttle leave for Armstrong?" Pauline removed her hand. "In about fifteen hours," she said, looking disappointed. "Could you arrange for two passengers to travel without being manifested?" Pauline turned back to her console, "If it's about this CIS business, I don't want to become involved."

She turned again to face him "Anyway, I'd lose my job if I pulled a stunt like that."

Stone took her hand. "Listen, Pauline, this is world shattering stuff. I can't tell you exactly what we're about, but if we don't manage to get to Armstrong unannounced, you may not have a job in a few months."

"How do I know what you're telling me is the truth?" she said

Stone looked over to Susan and nodded. She came over to where they were sitting and pulled up a chair. "Hello, I'm Agent Stone." Pauline looked her over, "Same name, a coincidence, yes?" Susan gave her a direct stare leaning closer. "No, I'm his wife. I don't know what else my husband has told you, but you can believe that!" "He ain't told me jack, lady."

"Then maybe I can help. I'm a courier from CIS and I have recently brought information that makes it imperative that we get to Luna, without being detected." Susan produced her card; the Captain took it, then wiped it through her machine. The machine confirmed Susan's identity.

Hicks sat back in her chair, a serious look passing over her face. "Let me think about this then I'll contact you within the next four hours, ok?"

Susan squeezed her hand. "Thank you, you won't regret it."

"I may, Honey ... I may."

They left the Captain sitting at the console and headed for the elevators, halting in front of the door marked *Passengers*. Stone looked at the ceiling as they rode the elevator to their room. Susan suddenly turned to him. "Nice lady, Stone." She was glaring at him.

Stone looked puzzled, "Yes I suppose so." "Are you sure you've told me everything about your trip?" queried Susan. "Of course, she just helped me when I was doped up. Why." Susan pursed her lips and remained silent. The door opened to their room and she entered ahead of Stone, Springfield was waiting for them.

"How did things go?"

"Humph!" said Susan

Stone looked over her head at Springfield with a quizzical look, and shrugged.

"Oooooh, that good ......" said Springfield sweetly.

"We have to wait for her answer," said Susan. "But judging by the way she and my husband behaved, I think we're safe."

Springfield stood and stretched. "I think I'll just go for a walk." He left in a hurry smiling to himself.

"Any more surprises, Harry?" she said, taking off her shoes.

"What do you mean?"

"I mean, do you have any other women fawning all over you." She looked angry, then seeing his confusion she laughed, "Come here, lover boy."

At that moment the door chimed announcing the arrival of the young room service attendant.

"I did as you asked, Mr Stone. My boss has permanently allocated me to your room." She smiled beautifully. Susan glared at Stone and opened her mouth to speak ....

CHAPTER 6

"**N**o way!" Springfield was sitting opposite Stone. The remnants of lunch lay between them. Stone sat back. "Charlie, I have nobody else I can trust. You will have to go and get the information from Stevens!"

Springfield stood up, "And who's going to look after you?" Stone looked across at his wife and inclined his head, "The tame Amazon here. We've already discussed it."

Springfield stood up and picked up his glass. He turned towards the big window facing out onto the Earth. He stared at his glass for a few seconds then drained the contents. "I guess you're right, but I still don't like the idea of splitting our forces."

Stone rose and crossed to the big man, "Look, Charlie, I don't like the idea either, but I need you to run a trace on our five suspects and also to find Miles. Additionally I need you to do some digging and see if you can stir the pot a little to see what emerges ....Ok?"

Springfield's shoulders appeared to slump, "Ok, Harry but as soon as I think fit I'm heading out to Luna."

Springfield reached into his pocket and took out a small metal cube, "Roll up your sleeve."

Stone looked at him for a moment, then complied. Springfield placed the device over the exposed forearm and pressed down, resulting in a loud click. Stone jumped and snatched his arm away, "What the bloody hell! ..." He looked down at his forearm, all he could see was a puncture mark centred on a small lump under his skin. Stone looked up. "What on god's Earth was that?"

Springfield smiled, "You don't need to know. In fact, better you don't, then you can't tell anyone." He paused and looked thoughtful, "All you need to know is, if you are ever in real trouble press the lump very hard with a fingernail. Remember, very hard." He reached into his pocket again and took out a bracelet. "Put this on your wrist, it's a tracer."

Picking up his notebook, he shook hands with Stone, gave Susan a hug and then without a further word strode to the door.

The room appeared empty without the big man's presence. Susan crossed to Stone and put her arms around his waist and pulled him towards her. "How long before we have to leave?" Stone looked down and wrapped his arms around her shoulders. "About half an hour. Hicks said that she would call when she was ready for us." They stood locked in each other's embrace for a long time. Then Susan, suddenly all businesslike, pushed away and smiled. "Just like old times, eh!" She disengaged from his arms and left the room. Stone went to the desk computer, called up his list and was about to start an analysis sequence when the door chimed announcing a visitor.

A worried looking Captain Hicks entered carrying a flight bag which she dropped to the floor. "Don't worry," said Stone holding both her hands, "everything will be Ok." "That's Ok for you to say, your job isn't riding on this," she replied. Just then Susan appeared. She looked at them, was about to say something, then looked at Pauline's face and thought better of it Instead she smiled, "Everything will be all right, Captain, I promise." Pauline pulled her hands away, and turned to Susan. "Sure it will!" she smiled. "You're a lucky lady, he's a nice catch." Susan stepped forward and Stone jumped between the two women. "It's time to go, ladies!" Susan picked up her bag and headed towards the door. Pauline gave Stone a big smile and looking at Susan's back, shrugged and mouthed an obscenity. Then reached into her flight bag. "When we get to the loading bay, I want you both to put these on." She held out a pair of white plastic coveralls with attached hoods. "Then, collect my kit which will be by the elevator and follow me into the control room, I'll take it from there." She looked from one to the other. "Remember, on my ship I'm the Captain. Understood?" She looked at Susan. Susan glared back, "Understood!"

ARMSTRONG BASE

The Manager stopped pacing for a moment. "What do you mean, you have authority? I'm the only one with the authority to allow entry!" She pointed at Stone, "and, Mister, I don't give you two that authority." She sat at her desk and looked from Susan to Stone. "You will both remain in your assigned quarters until the next shuttle out of here! Do I make myself clear?" The Manager's knuckles were white, "and as for that soon to be ex-employee pilot, she will be answering criminal charges."

Stone stood, "Is that all?" Before the Manager could reply, Susan was up and out of her chair, rounding on the Manager she said angrily, "I've got something to say to you about this!"

"Miss Stone!"

"Mrs Stone to you madam!" Pearson took a pace back, "What!"

"Look here Miz Pearson or whatever you are, we have just explained that there is a serious breach of security in your establishment, and all you can do is worry about some minor breach of transit regulations." Susan brushed her hair back from her face and stepped back, her face flushed with anger.

"I'm the Base Manager here Mrs Stone, and as such am answerable only to my company; and travel without authority between any planets or facilities is illegal. I don't make the laws, but will I damned well enforce them!"

Stone moved forward and took his wife's arm. "Come on dear, it's time we stopped wasting the Manager's time." Susan was still furious and pulled her arm away. "Are you letting her get away with this?" Stone sighed "I don't see what else we can do." Susan gave him a withering look and stormed from the office, nearly knocking down a worried looking Shuttle pilot who was waiting to enter.

Stone turned to Pearson, "Are you quite sure that you wish to take this line of action?"

The Manager looked thoughtful for a moment then said in a quiet voice, "I have no choice. Goodbye Mr, Stone." Stone turned to leave just as Pauline entered. She stared at him and he looked away. "Thanks, pal. See you in the labour office!" Stone left in a hurry.

Back in their room, Stone poured himself a drink of local whisky. Then he sat looking at his wife's back as she fussed with the bedcovers. He said quietly, "That was not a good time for a confrontation." She turned on him, "Then when is the time? After this place goes up in smoke?" "That's not likely to happen," he said calmly.

She was becoming unreasonable and she knew it but the frustration was too much. "I gave my word to that Shuttle Pilot, you are so fond of … Now look what's happened!"

Stone held up a finger and beckoned to her. She crossed to him looking puzzled and he whispered in her ear, "I've turned on the *DEBUG,* now we can talk safely."

She threw her arms around his neck and in a loud voice said, "I'm sorry, Honey." Then whispered, "What's the range?"

He looked down at her and answered softly, "About ten inches, at less than 10 db." She nodded and leant closer, "Where do we go from here?"

"I suggest we look up the Security Chief and see where he stands. When I was here last he seemed to be Ok and we have to trust someone."

At that moment, the ground shook and the lights flickered once, twice, then went out. Immediately the low-power emergency lights came on, bathing the area in a dim yellow glow. After what seemed an eternity the main lights resumed. Stone sighed with relief. "What the hell was that?" Suddenly a siren wailed some distance away, followed by excited shouting and the sound of running feet.

Stone started to move towards the door "Come on, I think things may have started already!"

They raced down the narrow corridor towards the Manager's office, but nobody was there. Everyone in sight was hurrying towards the shuttle bay. Stone grabbed the arm of a passing man. "What's going on?" The man pulled his arm away and continued to run, shouting over his shoulder as he went, "Something to do with the Shuttle, an accident I think!" Stone turned to his wife, "Come on, I hope it's not Pauline!" They both headed down the passage towards the shuttle bay.

The scene was one of chaos, with people running everywhere. He spotted the Manager and headed towards her, "What gives Pearson?" She turned on him angrily, faced flushed. "What the hell are you doing here, you are supposed to be confined to your quarters!" Stone grabbed her arm, "This is an emergency I take it?"

"Yes, so why don't you stay out of the way and let us get on with our jobs!" She turned towards the exit. Stone got in front of her, "Look here, Pearson, if what I think has happened, a friend of mine is involved … So, what can I do?" Pearson suddenly appeared to deflate. "I'm sorry. Look, go to the Chief Engineer over there and see what he needs. Then come back and see me!" She pointed to a man dressed in bright yellow coveralls. Stone had already gone towards him recognising a man he had interviewed on his earlier visit. Susan stared at Pearson, who briefly held her gaze, then looked away. After a brief pause Susan went over to where Stone was standing talking to the Engineer. "Susan, this is Max Shroader. He tells me that there was a failure in the field coil control system. Sector One coils fired just after they had loaded the shuttle back onto the launch rail. Apparently, not all the Shuttle's systems were ready to launch. Pauline was aboard when the Shuttle just took off and fell onto the roof of the shuttle bay. They are trying to get to her now." Susan looked grim, "Anything we can do?" The man called Max looked at her. "Not unless you can use a vacuum excavator. At the moment all we can do is wait her for the equipment to be set up outside the Shuttle's hatch." He wiped his brow, "We were lucky only one section was breached, at the loading platform." He pointed to the top of the escalator. For the first time, they noticed that the airlock doors were closed at the top of the ramp. "There's just vacuum behind there" said Max. "I'm not sure, but I think everyone got out before the doors sealed." Stone noticed the little man who had helped him on his first trip, and waved his arm. The man, seeing him, grinned and came over, "What are you doing back here, mate?"

Stone grabbed the man's shoulders, "Did you see the pilot?" The man's smile disappeared, "Man … I didn't see anything. I was too busy running for the doors. The first thing I knew was when the arse-end of the shuttle pushed through the wall. I just panicked and ran. Lucky I had just returned from outside and was still wearing a vacuum suit!"

Max had just finished talking on his phone. "They tell me that the Shuttle is in one piece, but is lying on its side just under the gantry so they can't get at the hatch just yet and will have to dig under to get at it." He looked grim. "They can see the pilot though the front port, she's in pretty bad shape. They say she looks as if she was caught standing during the acceleration, they can't tell yet if she is still alive. Sorry, pal."

Stone remembered Pearson's message. "The Manager wants to know if there is anything you need." Max looked at him, "I need a bloody miracle and some more vacuum qualified miners to help with the repairs!" Stone patted Pritchard's shoulder and turned to leave. "I'll see what I can do." "Thanks!" shouted Pritchard to his retreating back.

Susan caught up with him, "Harry, I'll stay here and see if I can be of any help." He paused, "Ok, but take care!" Giving her a quick kiss, he ran off down the corridor.

Susan turned and walked back to Max and tapped him on the shoulder. "Ok, where can I get a vacuum suit?" Pritchard looked at her. "I really don't need any more casualties at the moment." Susan smiled "I'm fully qualified in vacuum operations. I spent two years on the Mars run, and I'm an engineer. Just get me a suit, please."

"Ok, but be careful and don't get in the way." He spoke to an attendant, "Take the lady and get her fitted with a general purpose suit, then stay with her while she's topside." The man nodded and beckoned Susan to follow him.

"Just get as many miners to the Shuttle Bay as possible!" Pearson looked up and smiled at Stone. "Thanks, and sorry if I was a bit tetchy back there." Stone shrugged and returned the smile. "Understandable. Any idea what happened?"

"No idea yet, I'm waiting on a report from Max."

"I understand the pilot was aboard?" The Manager looked uncomfortable.

"So I hear, I don't know what the hell she was doing. Nobody is supposed to be aboard when the shuttle is being hoisted."

"I guess this drops the situation into CIS's lap," said Stone.

"Don't be stupid, this is company business. Why would an accident investigation interest CIS."

"This is the second accident to a shuttle in the last four months, isn't it? And if I'm not mistaken Senate funding accounts for a full third of operating costs."

"So what!"

"Well, that could constitute a Federal security threat, and as senior operative in place I could request CIS to send an investigation team or he paused and locked eyes with her,

"I could do the job myself if I was released, that is, from the previous unpleasantness ....What do you think?"

Pearson sat down and stared at her hands for a few moments. Suddenly she looked up and smiled, "I think that would be acceptable, providing I'm kept fully informed as to your progress."

"Of course." He stood, "Please could you tell the Security Chief that I will be paying him a visit."

Back in his quarters Stone made two quick calls; one to Karl Fisher, the Security Chief, and the other to his wife to tell her what was happening. It was then that he discovered that she was topside...

WASHINGTON DC

Springfield had been in town for less than two hours before he noticed that someone was following him. He had made arrangements to meet his contact at the Arlington Cemetery. It had been a long trip from the Cape and he was tired from the Shuttle flight. The gravity increase was bothering him a little. He'd only been away for four days and pitied the people who served for long periods off planet.

He caught the movement out of the corner of his eye. He had seen the man before either at the Airport or at some stage of the trip, he wasn't sure which.

I'm getting too old for this, he thought. He turned and looked straight at the man who was of medium build, dark hair, fair complexion and dressed in a smart one piece suit, 'Company' was written all over him. As the man turned away Springfield ducked behind a tree and waited. The man turned back and saw that his quarry had vanished. Panic spread across his face and he started to run.

Springfield grabbed him as he passed, one massive arm wrapped around the neck, and the other crossing through the forearm and up the man's back in a vicious hammer lock, Springfield's right foot jabbed at the back of the man's right knee, and he sagged down onto his knees, only supported only by his bent arm. There was a crunching crack, the man screamed. Springfield dumped him on his face and dropped his knee into the small of the man's back... Releasing his grip on the man's neck, Springfield quickly and expertly emptied a small arsenal of weapons onto the ground in front of him. When he was satisfied that the man was clean, he stepped back, allowing him to sit. Judging from the man's posture, Springfield knew that the arm was dislocated or broken.

"Put your feet straight out in front of you, and don't say anything!" The man complied, glaring at Springfield. He almost toppled but manage to get his left arm down to save himself. The right arm dropped and the man shouted an obscenity.

Tough guy, thought Springfield, squatting down in front of the man. "Who are you?" The man just stared. "Ok ... we can do this the hard way," said Springfield, getting up. The man looked wary. "How do you want it, left leg broken first, or the right?" He placed his foot on the knee of the extended right leg and pressed.

The man made a grab for the offending foot and fell backwards, the dislocated right arm hitting the ground underneath him. The man screamed, "Enough!" Springfield squatted in front of him again, "Who are you!?"

"Pendleton." the man replied, trying to sit upright.

"What do you want?" The man was silent for a moment and Springfield started to get up,

"I'm an operative just like you. Head of surveillance ordered a trace on you."

"Why?" Springfield asked.

"How I should know, you know how things are. I'm supposed to report where you go and who you see. Beyond that I know nothing," the man replied belligerently.

"Do you know who I am?" asked Springfield.

"Of course. They told me you were codenamed Springfield, a renegade officer who had managed to dump his trace."

"Do you believe that?"

You don't have a trace, do you? What am I supposed to think?"

"You have a point," said Springfield, getting up. "I'm going to relieve you of all this hardware and then you had better get to a hospital. I don't want to see you again. You're blown, you understand!" The man nodded. Springfield collected the weapons and left the man lying on the grass. "Next time, be more careful where you walk." The man looked up, but Springfield had gone.

Heading for the Arlington Memorial Springfield thought about what Pendleton had said. They know that I came to Earth, how..? The only people he could think of were Stone, his wife, and the ferry pilot. The only other possibility was him that he had been tracked before he got rid of the *personal trace*." He realised that he should have asked how Pendleton knew where to find him. Too late now! He thought.

A young woman passed in front of the Memorial, saw him and changed direction towards him. She rushed up and threw herself into his arms giving him a very passionate kiss. Then whispered into his ear, "Springfield?"

"Yes," he said gasping for breath.

"Thank god for that, I thought it was you by your photo."

"Lucky for you that I take a good picture, otherwise you would have had some explaining to do." She held onto him a moment longer, then releasing her hold on him, slipped a small package into his pocket. "That was the information that you asked for." she beamed a beautiful smile at him. "I was also told to tell you that Paul Miles had been found and recovered, but is in a bad way… He is safe though."

"You're new at this aren't you?"

"How did you know?"

"Call it instinct." He took her arm and they began to wander among the white headstones.

"Ottawa sent me and instructed me, not to contact the Washington office but to deliver direct to you."

Thanks, Steve! Springfield thought. He had asked his friend, Stevens the head of the Canadian office, to keep the investigation under wraps. It appeared that he had done this by appointing a very junior courier.

"Where can we go to read the chip?" he said looking for the tell-tale scar beneath her ear.

"That won't be necessary. I'm not rigged yet, my boss thought it would be safer because everyone knows I'm still in first year training. This is a simple data chip that will only play on your personal computer I'm to tell you, that you must key ... *'the date that we first met'*, whatever that means, otherwise the card will wipe."

Springfield thought for a moment and asked innocently, "By the way, how did you know where to find me?" She looked surprised, "Why, my boss told me you would be here for our meeting as arranged." "Did you tell anyone where you were going?" Springfield asked. "No. Oh, wait a minute ... when I was outside the airport I told the cab driver to bring me here, that's all." Springfield led her across the road from Arlington and placed her into a cab. "I don't know your name, but thanks. You're Ok." She dimpled at him, as the cab pulled away.

Springfield seated himself comfortably in his hire car and spoke to his computer, "Morning, Fred." *Morning, Guv*, came the cheerful response. "A little job for you, scan this card." Springfield pushed the card into the slot at the top of the machine and keyed in 12/3/2156. The computer's screen came to life and started to scroll line after line of information. The jumble of words and symbols were meaningless. Springfield waited until the scrolling had stopped. He looked at the last screen of information. The computer chimed "Please provide voiceprint answers to the following random questions:

Mother's first name...... "Naomi."

Registration number of current personal vehicle ..... "100445"

Name of primary education facility ….. "Roseville Primary"
Information available. Do you require hard copy or oral brief? ….."Oral brief, please, Fred."

The computer seemed to sigh … *Ok, here we go, the first on the list is* ……..

Vladimir Petrovic, Nuclear Power Engineer, married to Sacha Petrovic with three children, Grigori … male twenty two, Alexi, male twenty and Sofia, female fourteen. She and the children are currently living in Vladivostok, Mother and Father on both sides of the family are deceased. The wife works part time at the local office of the Lunar Exploration Company… a subsidiary of Transglobal … The two boys work as labourers at a local construction site owned by Transglobal and Sofia attends the local High School………

Rosemary Pearson, Site Manager Armstrong Base, works for Transglobal. Not married, no children. Parents currently living London, England. Both parents are retired……..

Maurice Haslop, Load Controller, married. Wife Christiane, no children. Wife is currently living in Washington DC. Works for the Department of Mining and Civil Engineering………….

Arnold Mason, Programmer, married with one son. Wife's name Sarah. Lives with her parents Simon Jones and Margaret Jones … in London Ontario Canada. Parents of Arnold Mason are deceased. Son's name is Martin aged 22. Wife does not work but Martin works for the Canadian Power Corporation a subsidiary of Transglobal………….

Lim Lee, Mining Tecnician, married, no children. Wife Ong, lives with her parents in Kuala Lumpur, Malaysia. Kim worked for Ipoh Mining, a subsidiary of Transglobal………..

Peter Thompson, System Analyst, married, no children. Wife Sandra lives with her parents in Richmond Virginia. Sandra works for ... you guessed it ... Transglobal.............

That's the lot, mate.... a detailed printout of the addresses to follow...... The little machine went silent.

Springfield sat back and thought about the information he'd been given. A stream of paper issued from the top of the machine. Springfield folded the paper and placed it in his pocket. Next he keyed in a series of numbers and spoke....." Fred, clean memory for all transactions in the last ten minutes."

Done, said the machine. Next, Springfield called the airport and booked a flight to Vladivostok. He then called the phone number on the little piece of paper. "Mrs. Petrovic?"

CHAPTER 7

ARMSTRONG BASE

The craft lay on its side like a beached whale. Stone could make little sense of the scene at first. Cables and steel scaffold surrounding the shuttle added to the confusion. The rescue party were just about ready to attach the lifting cables. A small figure standing on the hook end of a cable was being lowered onto the top of the shuttle. The hook had almost touched the metal surface when the figure eased itself off the end of the cable and guided the hook into the lifting ring. The figure then waved and the cable tightened. The whole structure moved. The figure staggered, then steadied itself by holding on to the cable. Slowly the back end of shuttle rose upwards until it cleared the ground by a few feet. Other suited figures rushed beneath it and placed supports on either side of the exposed hatchway. Stone could not see from the monitor who was involved, but he knew one of the white clad figures was his wife. He could hear her now and again over the radio but could not tell what she was doing.

The voice of the Engineer, Max, came clearly over the system, "Ok, have you got her?" "Not yet!" came the anonymous reply. "We are having a little trouble cycling the hatchway." The voice gasped as if under exertion, "That's got it, we just need some juice applied to the external power socket, ouch!" There was a short pause. "Right, it's in place, try the cycle switch now." A high-pitched whine sounded, followed by a loud hiss of escaping air. "Stop!" "Close it!" The panic in the voice was unmistakable, "The inner hatch has not sealed tight, it must have warped in the frame. I've just resealed the outer hatch door."

Max's voice was calm, "Now settle down, people. Let's think about this carefully." Susan's quiet voice sounded from the communicator. "How about rig a temporary pressure shelter and seal its universal connector against the Shuttle's hatch, then equalise the pressure."

"I knew I let you out there for something lady, Ok, let's get on with it."

"How much time do we have?" asked Susan.

"Don't know.... an hour... two, who knows?" answered Max.

An inflatable structure grew rapidly around the shuttle's passenger hatch, air lines were hooked up and the soft composite seal of the Universal Connector was pushed against the outer door. "We're in the shelter now and sealing it … Looks like we have a tight seal. Now we'll try to cycle the hatch. A clang sounded, followed by the whine of the Shuttle's outer hatch opening … "There's still pressure in here" called Susan. "I'm just entering the secondary hatch now." There was another whining noise, followed by a slight pop as the pressures equalised as she forcefully closed the inner hatch behind her, there was a shower of electrical sparks from the hatch control. "OK, I'm in the main cabin now and moving towards the control room." There was a slight tapping noise followed by a gasp. "I've found her. She's still breathing, but she's in a mess, bruises everywhere and losing blood from the nose!" A shuffling noise followed. Stone could hardly contain himself. "Will she be all right?" he asked. His wife breathing heavily, replied, "I really can't tell. I will need to get her suited up but we can't move her until I've checked for spinal injuries." After a while, her voice sounded strained, "I can't see anything obviously wrong. I'm just going to get her into her vacuum suit now," After a few minutes of laboured breathing and rustling sounds, Susan sighed. "Ok, she's suited up and air tight. I'll just take a quick look around before we leave." "Take care Honey," replied Stone.

Susan moved through the control room looking for something that might provide an answer. She noticed that the main board was active. She slipped into the pilot's chair and spoke into the on-board computer, there was no response. Max called over her headset, "Try using its alias ... *Dianne.*"

Susan tried again. "Dianne, systems report."

The on-board computer responded, *Systems malfunctions in the following areas, Life support has failed and CO_2 is approaching unacceptable high level. Drive system and control systems are inoperative. Minor breaches in hull integrity, auto-patched. Hatch 3 and cargo hatch are now inoperative.* The machine went silent. Susan leaned forward and flipped a switch on the console and the internal lights came on. "Dianne, what caused the systems to malfunction?" *The launch sequence was activated whilst the shuttle was being re-mated with the launch rail.* "Dianne, who activated the launch sequence?"

The computer answered, *I did.* Susan sat stunned for a moment

"Dianne, you did?" *Yes, on the orders of the pilot*

"Dianne, confirm that. You say the pilot ordered the launch sequence?"

Correct, the pilot used the manual override to negate the safety interlock system."

The computer sounded distressed, "I cautioned against launching, but was ordered to continue. Smoke started to pour from the console. *Fire warning in ....* The computer went silent and the lights went out. "Time to leave." thought Susan

"What's going on?" Stone had heard the computer's answer and the comment about fire.

"The computer has failed I'm out of here!" She said "We have a fire brewing in the control room. The firefighting system is down so I'll open the ship to vacuum." After checking the seals on their vacuum suits Susan manoeuvred the Captain to the inner passenger hatch a shiny object caught her eye. It was square piece of what looked like glass but it wasn't. Susan was looking at something very familiar. She placed the object inside her glove and resealed it to the suit. Smoke was now billowing from the flight deck. She closed a switch and air hissed out of the ship, her suit tightened about her body. She then tried to open the hatch, but it was jammed again. "Ok, I'm coming out now." Using the manual control she heaved on the door. She had forgotten that there was pressure on the other side of the hatch. There was a small explosion as the hatch slammed inwards. She jumped to one side, but the inrush of air hammered her against the bulkhead. The last thing she saw was a star-like crack on the face plate of her helmet and the suit started to go limp. "Bloody hell, what a way to go." she thought as her world went black.

8

GENEVA

"Where is he now?" asked the old man.

"I don't quite know, without a trace on him, we are having difficulty following his movements."

"Does he suspect us?"

"Possibly. After all, we don't know where Miles is either!"

"Could Springfield have him?"

"I doubt it. Springfield has been moving around too much to babysit a semi-cripple."

"This is all turning to shit." The old man came from behind his desk, "Set up a direct company flight to Luna. We are going to deal with this ourselves."

"Are you sure you're fit enough for a direct flight?"

"Of course I am. I may be old but I'm not feeble!" The old man turned to the window and gazed out on the neat gardens, his forehead creasing. "One mistake, one accident and months of planning wasted … the whole election campaign in jeopardy.

He turned again, angrily, "You're still here?" "Get on with it, man!"

ARMSTRONG BASE

"What the hell happened?" said Stone. "Not sure, give me a moment." Max replied.

The engineer turned to the communications console, "What's going on out there, guys?"

"The hatch just blew in, Boss," said a disembodied voice. "An explosive decompression we think. We're just recovering the people now, one suit is partially deflated," came the reply. "Everyone Ok?" Max asked.

"Can't tell at the moment. We have them at normal pressure now.

"Ok, wait there, I'll come and supervise."

"I'm moving them to Medical ASAP."

"Ok, keep me posted. I'll meet you at the main hatch," said Max.

"Ok, Boss, will do."

Stone turned and started for the Medical Centre. "I hope Susan is Ok,"

"She'll be all right," said Max, "Tough one, that wife of yours." Max turned towards the tunnel where the main hatch led into the Base.

Stone arrived at the medical treatment centre a couple of minutes before the two stretchers arrived, with Max following behind.

Stone found Susan on the first stretcher. He looked at the orderlies with an anxious expression.

"Don't panic, mate, I think she'll be fine. Just give us a few minutes to get her out of this lot. I'll be able to let you know more then," the orderly said, smiling in sympathy.

"What the hell is wrong with this place?" said Stone angrily. "Someone has turned incompetence into an art form!"

Both men sat down on the bench outside the treatment centre, Stone fidgeting with his computer but unable to concentrate. Max placed a comforting hand on his shoulder and spoke softly. "Don't worry, my friend, Dr Kline is a very experienced Flight Surgeon. He was on the Mars run for five years. She couldn't be in better hands."

Twenty minutes later the treatment centre door opened and a middle aged man appeared. He was medium height and build, dark hair going grey at the temples, but for all that he looked surprisingly fit. He stopped in in front of Stone,

"I'm the Base Medical Officer, Dr Kline. I take it from your reaction that the young lady is more than a colleague … yes?" "She is my wife," replied Stone.

"Oh, that explains it." The Doctor continued, "The young lady was very lucky, her suit only partially deflated. We would like to keep her under observation for a few hours. By then she should be ready for discharge." Dr Kline spoke soothingly, "She will have some slight discolouration of the skin due to burst minor blood vessels, but that should disappear over the next few days." The doctor paused. "Did you know the shuttle pilot?"

"Yes, but not very well; met her on the trip to Gamma 5, nice lady." "Why do you ask?"

The doctor sighed, "Well, she's a dead shuttle pilot now, fracture at the base of the skull and some major organ damage. Sorry, nothing I could do. She was dead on arrival." "I have to say she will be sadly missed. She was very popular on this base … a great chess player." Kline stood up, "I suppose you would like to see your wife now … yes?"

"Thank you," Stone responded. "That would be good". "I'll see you later, Boss," said Max and turned towards the Control Centre." "Thanks Max."

Stone walked through the doorway into a large brightly lit room. Six beds lined walls, three on each side. A set of monitoring and resuscitation instruments was placed next to each bed. Susan was lying in the last bed.

Stone moved to the side. He noticed that she was awake but she appeared sleepy.

"How are you, Honey?" he said taking her hand. She looked at him, wet her lips with her tongue, "I've been better Darling," she smiled, "but very happy to be here. I thought I was done for." Her face showed red burst capillary lines on her cheeks and under her eyes, but otherwise Stone thought she was the most beautiful sight in the whole universe. "The doctor says you can come home today," he said. "That will be good." She turned her head away from him so that he could not see the tears running down her face. "I will look forward to that. Is Pauline all right?" Stone suddenly realised that she had not been told about the pilot. He thought for a moment, then said, "Sorry, Honey she didn't make it, her injuries were too extensive. Apart from that, the doc said that she was dead on arrival at the centre."

His wife looked puzzled but said nothing. Stone felt awkward, perhaps he shouldn't have said anything. "Look, Honey you get some sleep now, I'll come back in a couple of hours." She smiled as he bent and kissed her forehead, "Love you." Stone left the treatment room and headed for the Control Centre.

Stone arrived at the Control Centre as the outside crews were raising the damaged shuttle away from the launch rail. Repairs could only begin when the space craft was back in the maintenance hangar.

Stone looked for Max and found him deep in discussion with several Shuttle engineers, who obviously had just returned from the surface as they were still wearing the lower halves of their vacuum suits. Max addressed the group. "So there is some major structural damage, but not irreparable ... Yes?" One of the engineers who had appointed himself spokesman replied.

"That's about the sum of it, but we still can't be sure that there are no hidden fracture lines. It will take us about two weeks to go over the whole of the shuttle's frame." Max thought for a moment, "I guess that that means we will have to fly the backup shuttle to continue operations."

"I guess so," said the spokesman whose name was Thomas, he continued. "But in the meantime what do we do about the bent guide rail? We can't launch anything until we replace about a thirty metre section." "We can still land shuttles, of course, but we can't turn them round on this accelerator. Maybe we can use the government's interplanetary launch facility. It's a possibility and not far from here."

At this point Stone lost interest in the engineering discussion and walked away, deciding not to bother Max for the moment. He headed towards the Manager's office.

He arrived at the office just as Fisher, the Security Chief, was leaving, looking furious.

"Bloody woman!" he choked. "How many more people have to die here before she gets off her arse?" He looked at Stone. "Best of luck with this one, incidents she calls them, bloody incidents. I suppose a nuclear war is just a Sunday event to that bitch!" He stormed off leaving Stone with his hand on the door handle. Stone was about to knock on the door and changed his mind. He turned and followed the Security Chief.

Fisher had just sat down at his desk when Stone entered. "Can I have a word?" Stone asked. "I guess you must be the illegal immigrant that she's being whining about for the last few days. We've met before." He waved his hand, indicating Stone to take the seat on the couch next to the door. "Coffee?"

"Thanks, but do you have anything stronger? I think I need it at this moment." Fisher went to a cabinet and poured two large drinks, "Bourbon do?" He handed a drink to Stone, "Not the local crap we get here, but good imported Tennessee, costs a fortune." Stone took a mouthful,

"Thank you, I really needed that." Fisher sat behind his desk and took a small sip, leaned back and waited. Stone lowered his voice. "Yes, and we have met before, I was here last week, interviewing Company employees." "Is this room *voice secure*?" Fisher pressed a button on his desk, "It is now" he said. "Good. What I have to tell you may place you under certain obligations to the Earth Senate." Stone took another drink, "I and the other illegal immigrant, for want of a better word, are in reality agents for CIS. I am an analyst, and my partner is a Field Operative." He decided to bend the truth a little with regards to Susan's actual status. "Are you aware that my partner was injured during the last shuttle incident?" "Yes, so I heard when I spoke to the Chief Engineer." "At that time things were pretty chaotic, so I decided to leave further questioning until things settled down a bit.

What do you know about a man that disappeared four months ago, just before the first shuttle accident?" "All I know is, that his name was Carlsen and he was a maintenance engineer. He disappeared a couple of weeks after the Reactor incident, and before the Shuttle Crash that shut launches down for ten days." Fisher took another drink. "Interestingly, one of our other maintenance workers died of a supposed heart attack shortly after the Reactor incident."

"Supposed heart attack? There was no post mortem?" asked Stone

"Sure there was, but the bitch refused me access to the findings, said the results were consistent with heart attack and that I should leave well enough alone." Fisher got up and refilled his glass, "Of course, I thought her behaviour was extraordinary and I had her watched." Fisher sat down again. "I spoke to the Medical Officer who performed the Autopsy. He confirmed what the Manager had said, but he did add one interesting item. He said that the man appeared fit and he could find no evidence of cardiac necrosis, ischemia or emboli. Basically the man's heart had just stopped."

"Had a toxicology screening test been requested?" asked Stone. Fisher leaned back in his chair and put his fingertips together.

"I asked just that question. The doctor told me he had, of course, sent samples to Earth for analysis and was waiting for the results."

"And the results were negative?" asked Stone,

"I don't know," said Fisher. "I have been unable to obtain the findings because the doctor was posted onto the Mars run two weeks later and nobody seems to be able to locate them. I contacted the hospital where the specimens were sent, and while they remember the specimens arriving at the laboratory, they were unable to find the results or the specimens themselves. They claim a computer malfunction."

"Interesting," said Stone. "I think it's time we spoke to the Base Manager together, don't you? "Absolutely." said Fisher, "Now?"

"No, tomorrow morning will be Ok. I have to check on my partner right now." Stone got up,

"Thanks for the drink." "No problem. Say, about 0830 tomorrow then?" said Fisher rising from his chair. "Sounds good," replied Stone as he reached for the door handle, suddenly he had a thought. "Did everyone on the base know that my partner was also my wife?"

"Not that I know. I certainly didn't until just now, hope she's Ok. Is she really a field agent?"

"She sure is," replied Stone grinning, "She sure as hell is!" He left the room still smiling.

Stone walked into the medical centre, looking for Susan. The curtains were drawn around her bed. Stone beckoned to an orderly, "Mrs Stone here?" he asked.

"Yes sir, she is just dressing. We wanted to keep her another twenty four hours, but she is a strong woman and insisted on leaving tonight." "That would be right," said Stone.

Just then Susan stepped from behind the curtains. "Hi, Honey, ready to go home?"

"If you are up to it, sure." She hooked her arm into Stones elbow and started for the door, stopped and spoke to the orderly, "Thank Doctor Kline for me. Tell him that I promise to come back tomorrow for a check-up." "Ok, Ma'am," he replied.

On arriving in their room they made love, not the sweet gentle act of lovers, but a violent kind of passion borne of fear and relief. Afterwards, they lay exhausted still, their bodies close and clinging, her leg across his stomach. With her head was on his shoulder, she looked up into his face. She almost had a compulsion to talk.

"I'm so sorry about Pauline," she said. "I liked her in a weird sort of way and they tell me she was a very good pilot." She propped herself on one elbow, looking him in the eye, "When I found her in the Shuttle, she was in a bad way, but I didn't think she was that bad. at least she looked reasonable when I got her to the hatch." She looked puzzled, "I don't understand, I examined her neck carefully before I suited her up and there certainly was no evidence of a fracture at the base of the skull. But then, I'm not a doctor, I suppose." Remembering the piece of chip she had found on the floor, "Did anyone give you a piece of crystal?" She sat up. "It would have been in my glove. I found it on the flood in the Shuttle." "Nobody gave me anything. You were still wearing your suit when they brought you in." replied Stone. "Then it must still be in the suit. We have to go and get it now," she replied forcefully. "Come on Honey!" She got up and pulled on her jumpsuit. Stone followed her lead. He was a bit disappointed, he'd been hoping for another round of passion…

When they arrived at the medical centre, another orderly was on duty. Susan walked up to the man, "Have you seen the vacuum suit that I was wearing today when they brought me in?" she demanded. The orderly looked mildly alarmed, thinking he was in trouble,

"No, Ma'am, I've just come on duty," he said. "Where do they usually put patients' property?" she asked. "There is a storeroom through there," replied the Orderly, pointing to a door at the far end of the treatment room. Moving to the door she flung it open, and stepped into a room that had a multitude of shelves and racks. She searched the room thoroughly... no suit. "Damn!" she said," She turned on the worried orderly, "Where else?" The orderly thought for a moment, "Was the suit Company property, Ma'am?" he said. "Of course," replied Susan with studied patience. "In that case it would have been returned to the Stores Office," he said with relief, having determined that he wasn't to blame.

"I know where that is" said Stone, "Let's go." They left the Medical Centre and walked quickly towards the control room end of the Base. Just before the Control Centre was a door marked Stores. They entered together, a clerk, sitting behind a computer console, looked up in surprise at the intrusion.

"Store's closed until 0800 tomorrow," he said with disinterest and looked back at the computer console. "This is really important," said Susan sweetly, "We just need look at the vacuum suit I was wearing today." Susan had recognised the clerk for what he was, obstructive and officious. She dimpled at him and offered her most seductive look, "Please .... It won't take us long, the suite number is VS 417, can't you look for me ...*please*." the clerk smiled and got up.

"Ok just for you Darling," He went into the adjoining room and a few minutes later emerged with the suit. "The helmet is busted," he said, "If you were wearing this you are one lucky lady." He handed the suit over and took off the attached gloves, Susan looked in the left hand glove, smiled and produced the chip. "Thank god," she said. "Thank you. What's your name?" "Frank," replied the clerk,

"Thanks, Frank. I'll remember your kindness," They left Frank wondering just what he had done that was so special, but smiling happily as returned his attention to his computer.

On arriving at their room they quickly examined the crystal chip.

"It's part of a recording chip," said Stone, "most likely from the music PA system."

"Probably ejected from the system when the Shuttle crashed. But where is the rest of it?" "Still in the machine?" suggested Stone. Susan interrupted him, "I have an idea. I wonder if we can read what is on this piece. Most of it is here. Let's try it in the room player." Then, placing the broken chip in the slot and making sure it was orientated correctly, she pressed play. There was a garble of noise, followed by bits of music, then broken fragments of Pauline's voice. "P…mis,…. Launch….."

Then clear as a bell, came the Flight Controller's voice, "Permission to launch ….. wi…dow…" followed by the pilot's voice, "Ok, Dia…a ….l a…..ch…," There was a four second delay the broken pieces of music continued in the background. Then clearly came the command in Pauline's voice "Launch!"

They both sat down, "Bastards!" said Susan. "They used a recording from a previous launch to trigger the on-board computer. Pauline didn't have a chance."

"Yes, but before voice commands can be used the pilot has to initialise the computer by pressing the launch sequence button. Pauline must have pressed that button, she was the only person aboard." "Right … but what could induce Pauline to press the button, and why would she do that?" "What we do know," said Stone, "is that this is not an accident nor a suicidal gesture by the pilot. This was a deliberate act of murder and sabotage."

CHAPTER 9

ARMSTRONG BASE

Next Morning, Susan suggested that they should brief Fisher, the Security Chief, on their discoveries, and then together proceed to confront the Manager. Shortly after finishing their breakfast they arrived at Fisher's office, knocked and entered.

"Morning, Karl," said Stone. Fisher got up from his desk and came round to greet them, heading straight for Susan he smiled, "And this must be the beautiful Mrs. Stone?" Susan smiled, she was used to this kind of greeting.

"I certainly am," she beamed at him. "Now we have been introduced, can we get down to business?" Fisher smiled back, "Of course. Susan sat while Stone spoke earnestly. Fisher's face changed from a relaxed expression to one of alarm. After several minutes Fisher broke in,

"You're telling me that someone on this Base is deliberately committing sabotage and murder. Do I hear right?"

"Yes!" said Stone and Susan together."

"Bloody hell," said Fisher, "Where to start looking?"

"We start with the senior executive and work our way down," suggested Susan, then added, "The questions are, who can install a false recording into the Shuttle's PA system, and who could convince the Pilot to initiate the launch sequence while the Shuttle is still loading. Also, who arranged to override the safety cut-outs that monitor the ready state of the Shuttle?" Stone thought for a moment,

"It has to be a person or a group that have routine access to launch control and maintenance systems." "Surely they have maintenance records?" said Susan. "I'll get one of my boys to check that out," Fisher replied. "What do you plan to do next?"

"I think it's time we all visited the dragon lady, don't you?" smiled Stone rising from his chair and leading the way ….

"What is the meaning of this intrusion!" demanded a very irate Base Manager rising from her chair. They had entered without knocking. All three sat down in front of the Manager's desk.

"That is what we would like to know," said Susan sweetly. "I am at a loss where to begin. First a Shuttle crashes four months ago and we are still waiting for a report on the cause of the incident, then there is yet another Shuttle accident," Susan leaned forward in her seat, "Miz Pearson, I am at a loss as to why the service was not shut down after the first incident? Can you at least answer that question?"

Pearson sat, staring at the trio for some seconds. "I don't know who you think you are bursting into my office like this, you have no authority from either my Company or a warrant from the Earth Senate, and therefore you have no authority!"

Stone rose from his chair and leaned over the Manager's desk, a threatening expression on his face. "One … I have the authority to conduct investigations into an organisation that has threatened to shut down mining on the Moon. Two … My partner has brought information from CIS Trends Division that the threat is credible, and that I personally may be in danger if I return to Earth. Three … one of our CIS Officers has disappeared on your Base and Four … what about the missing autopsy report on one of your men that died immediately after what appears to be a minor sabotage to your reactor." He straightened up and smiled. "And I, as senior CIS operative, think that that gives me sufficient authority to at least ensure the safety of this facility, don't you?" Pearson had gone pale, and appeared to be near tears. "But the man died of a heart attack, the doctor said so!"

"A perfectly heathy man in the prime of his life, and you think that this diagnosis, without a full pathology report, is valid? Also, why did you block Security from accessing the autopsy report?"

Pearson had her face in her hands, tears leaking between her fingers, "What do you want from me? I have been instructed by my bosses that I am to minimise the fallout to protect company interests. Also the first shuttle was scattered over a very wide area and not all the wreckage has been located. so a complete report may be months or even a year away." The statement sounded genuine to Stone, so he concentrated on the last incident.

"You are aware, are you not, that the pilot appeared to give the launch order?" "Yes, Engineering said they have a voice cockpit recording of her giving the order and the voiceprint identifies the speaker as Capt. Hicks" "Would it interest you to know that she did not order the launch? A recording playing from the PA system was actually the culprit. And according to my partner, that pilot was alive and comparatively intact when she was placed into a vacuum suit."

Pearson looked grief stricken, "They told me she was already dead when they took her from the hatch," she sobbed. Stone relented a little, "Listen Miss Pearson … It is Miss, is it not?"

"Yes," "Then let's get down to what you do know, then we may just confide in you, Ok?"

"First question … do you have any idea what caused the first accident?" Pearson dried her eyes with a tissue and sniffed, "The Engineering Department said that there appeared to be a major malfunction in the coil firing sequence just before the shuttle reached its launching point. Apparently the Shuttle had decelerated to less than two thirds its launch speed. When it left the launch rail it couldn't even maintain its correct attitude and when the emergency boosters fired it was already in a nose down position, causing the shuttle to power into the surface. As to what caused it, nobody yet can say; all of the computers check out. There is not much left to collect as evidence, and there is certainly no sign of the pilot's body."

"And what about the reactor malfunction?" Queried Susan.

Pearson sat up, looking a little more composed, "The Nuclear Engineer reported that a small section of coolant piping had blown out and that it was probably due to an over-pressure in an undetected weak spot in the pipe. The reactor was shut down for three days while repairs were made. This is an early Russian reactor, donated to the Company by one of its Russian subsidiaries. This of course was installed prior to 2125, so its not surprising when you consider the age of the unit. We had planned on decommissioning the plant this year and upgrading to a fusion unit, but the company baulked at the cost and delayed until next year." She shrugged, "I don't understand why the delay, raw fuel for a fusion reactor is Helium-3 and that is our primary export to Earth. But as in all organisation, the bean-counters rule." She leaned back in her chair, "Is that all?"

"One more question said Stone, "What do you know about the disappearance of a maintenance worker name Carlsen? You must have heard something.The worker, by the way, was one of our better field agents?" Again Pearson looked startled, "You had an agent here, without informing me?" "Yes, there's not much point in security if we tell everyone about it, is there?" "I suppose not," she replied sullenly. "All I know is that he was a recently arrived employee. I interviewed him, of course, and then Fisher here reported him missing."

"When exactly was this?" "Just before the Shuttle accident," she replied. Stone relaxed and smiled. "Thank you, Miss Pearson, you have been most illuminating."

He now understood what Miles had referred to when he told Springfield that he had given all the information needed to make an intuitive leap.

"For your information, Miss Pearson, I think I now understand what is going on and how. The questions remaining is why and who?" He moved towards the door beckoning Fisher to follow him, and spoke softly.

"Your turn, it's time you took control of this shambles. Brief her on what we have found. Use your judgement on details, but be careful, somehow she is mixed up in this …" he raised his voice, "Let's go Susan we'll go back to the control room briefly, then to our apartment." He quietly added to Fisher. "Get one of your men to watch her and monitor her calls." "Already done." said Fisher."

GAMMA 5

The two men headed for the Shuttle hangar, the younger one carrying a fairly large shoulder bag which was difficult to manage in the near zero gravity of the central hub. The elder man asked, "How long before we reach Armstrong?" His companion hoisted the bag higher onto his shoulder and replied, "About 20 hours, including wait time." "That's not too long. When we get there, I'll explain that we're on an inspection tour for the Board Meeting next month, got it? You are here representing CIS in an investigation of the Shuttle incident." The younger man nodded, "Sounds good."

The two men were in fact both senior Executives, Henry Dixon, a Chief Superintendent in CIS, the other one Alan Goldberg Vice President of Transglobal. The latter asked, "Do the operatives know you personally?" "No, not by sight, CIS has over one million employees on Earth alone it's most unlikely that we would have met. This Pearson woman, is she reliable?" "I'd say so, she has much to lose," replied the older man.

ARMSTRONG BASE

Susan and Stone arrived at the Control Centre to be greeted by Max Schroeder whom Stone had interviewed on his previous visit. Susan recognised a man of average build with blond hair and blue eyes, which gave the impression of a friendly and pleasant character. Stone had told her that he was unmarried and a career aerospace engineer who had been with the company for ten years, a solid citizen. However there was a lurking doubt in Stones mind that needed to be clarified. Hi Max you've met my partner, Susan?" Of course, at the accident. I'd like to thank you Susan, you don't mind me calling you that do you?" "Not at all," she replied. "That was really quick thinking with the temporary pressure hatch. Sad about the pilot though." "Yes, a good pilot; and I suspect, a good person." said Susan.

Stone cut in, "Max, there is something I need to ask you, who told you that Susan was my wife?" "You did." replied Max" "Ah yes, so I did," pressing his hand to his forehead, "Clean forgot, I remember now, telling you at the Clinic." "Right," said Max smiling. "How are the repairs to the track going?" asked Stone, changing the subject. "Progressing, the government launcher had spare sections, they have promised to lend them to us while we make new ones at the foundry." "Excellent. That means there will be little delay before the next launch, yes?" Max shook his head, "We still have to get the backup Shuttle out of mothballs and set it up to double as a cargo and passenger craft, purely as a temporary measure while we repair the damaged one." "How long will that take?" asked Stone.

"Oh, maybe six or seven days at the most, depending upon good breaks." Stone thought for a moment then said, "I can see you're busy, can I swing by later? I've got a couple of questions about the first shuttle crash that I'd like to float by you." "No problems," the engineer replied. "Ok, Max. See you later."

When they reached their quarters Susan looked questioningly at her husband. "Ok, what was all that about?" "It may be nothing, but do you remember what Max said about how he first found out about you being my wife. He said that he learned it from me at Medical. Well before then, when you were injured and still inside the shuttle, he said, "That wife of yours is a tough one." Stone turned and looked at his wife, "That's strange, because according to him, at that stage, I hadn't told him. I think I will have to look at our friend Max more carefully. I'll get Fisher to see what he can find out about him."

Fisher was just leaving his office when Stone arrived, "Hi, Karl, a little word with you if may?" "Sure," said Karl

"Karl, what do you know about Max Schroeder?" "Very little, except of course what is in his Security file ... He is an aerospace engineer, who has been with the company for 10 years. Why?" "It's just that he appeared to know more about me than an engineer should. For instance, he appeared to know that Susan was my wife. The information would only be available to the Manager and the Pilot. Even you didn't know, at that stage."

Fisher looked thoughtful, "That true, I didn't know until you told me. What do you want me to do?" Stone thought for a moment, "Perhaps you could request further information from the Personnel Office on Earth, but be careful how you word the request." "Consider it done." Fisher snapped his fingers, "Just remembered … While I was speaking to Pearson, she told me that she was expecting a visit from Alan Goldberg, the Vice President of Transglobal, and that accompanying him was some senior officer from CIS … I'm guessing but it's probably something to do with the last shuttle disaster." Stone stopped in the doorway and turned to face Fisher, "You say a senior CIS agent is with him? Do you know the agent's name?" "Yes, Pearson said that the agent was a Chief Superintendent by the name of Henry Dixon. Do you know him?" "Hardly," said Stone. "There are over a million agents situated on Earth … it would be unlikely for us to have met. I usually work out of a small unit in Singapore. If Dixon is travelling with the 'Brass' from Transglobal, I'm guessing that he works out of Geneva … Interesting though. Maybe I should call Ottawa to find out who he is, before he gets here." Fisher walked to the door, "Look, I have to do my rounds now. Can we meet later? Maybe I'll have some more information on our friends then," "Catch you later."

GAMMA 5

After catching the morning Shuttle from Earth, Springfield had decided to delay his departure from Gamma 5. He reasoned that he needed more time to collate the information he had gathered from Mrs. Petrovic. He did not wish to transmit this information because he didn't trust the security of the microwave link to Armstrong. In his head alarm bells were ringing furiously. After his visit to Mrs Petrovic he interviewed the rest of the families remaining on his list. Each interview provided new pieces of information that reinforced his concern. The good news was that Stevens had found Miles in Montreal General Hospital. He had apparently been picked up wandering the streets of that city. However, at the time he was unable to talk to anyone and appeared to have lost his memory entirely. The Ottawa Office had him under strict security At least there was one less thing to worry about. He wondered how Stone was getting along. He had just heard about the latest shuttle incident. The Company and the Senate were keeping the details of the accident close to their chests. He couldn't think why, it was bound to get out sooner or later. He shrugged, closing the door to his room. He had just decided that he would catch tomorrow's Shuttle to Armstrong, but now, he thought, there was just enough time for a beer before dinner.

ARMSTRONG BASE

The Shuttle had landed and was unloading its passengers into the arrival complex. Goldberg and Dixon walked to the desk where a reception committee was waiting. Goldberg extended his hand, "Hello, you must be Miss Pearson, the Base Manager, I've heard a lot about you. I'm Alan Goldberg, and this is Chief Superintendent Henry Dixon, a CIS officer." Dixon shook hands. "Nice to meet you Miss Pearson."

"Welcome to Armstrong Mr. Goldberg, and also to you, Chief Superintendent." She stepped back and indicated to them to follow her, then turned to the man standing next to her, "The Vice President's bags, John. Please follow me, gentlemen, we have your rooms ready for you." Goldberg nodded. "Thank you … may I call you Rosemary?" "Of course sir. Would you like to clean up before your meal?" "No, that won't be necessary, Rosemary, first things first. I was hoping that you could brief me and my colleague here on the progress that has been made regarding our current problems. I have, of course reviewed your reports, but I find it an advantage to hear details from the horse's mouth, so to speak," he smiled. "Of course, sir, if we could go to my office we can be sure of not being interrupted." "Thank you, that would be perfect, please lead on."

When they had returned to their room from their visit to the Security Chief, Stone and Susan discovered a message telling them to report to the Base Manager. They arrived at the office at the same time as Fisher who was carrying a large plastic folder under one arm.

"You too?" Stone enquired, "Yeah, she wants me along with all relevant information on our investigations." He opened the file and selected a plastic sheet and gave it to Stone, "This is the information you wanted on Max Schroeder, an interesting history. By the way, my Sergeant tells me that Max and Pearson, appeared to have a closer than usual relationship. Probably nothing, but who knows?" Fisher paused, "Also it's interesting that the Flight Controller and Max go back a long way." "That is interesting," said Stone slowly.

They entered the office together. Pearson was seated behind her desk. When they halted in front of her, none of them registered the men sitting on the couch behind the door. "You must be Stone." said a voice. Stone spun round and recognised the features of Alan Goldberg, Transglobal's Vice President. Seated next to him was a man that he did not recognise. Goldberg rose from his seat and extended his hand. Pearson stood and said, "Sir, may I also introduce, Miss Susan Stone, and the Chief Security Officer Karl Fisher."

The other man stood, "And may I introduce Chief Superintendent Henry Dixon," said Goldberg. "Sir," responded Stone, proffering his hand. "Glad to have another CIS officer on site. Perhaps we can get together later?"

"That won't be necessary, Stone," said the man coldly. "I have already been briefed by the Base Manager. She says that you arrived on the Base illegally and have repeatedly involved yourself in Transglobal matters that are of little concern to CIS, especially with respect to the investigations regarding the reactor incident and the two Shuttle accidents. These are more than likely an engineering or a procedural problem, rather than criminal in nature. I have to say that I am concerned that CIS may be overstepping its Senatorial Authority."

"I doubt that, sir. I have a clear mandate from the Ottawa Office to investigate a threat from an organisation styling itself the *Lunar Protection Society*. That in itself allows me to at least pursue several lines of investigation, including possible sabotage of Lunar installations."

"You could be right. However, as senior officer on site, I believe that there is potential for a mishandled investigation which could adversely affect the Company's operations." Dixon turned to the Vice President, "Mr Goldberg, as I discussed with you previously, I am the senior officer and I will assume responsibility for all future investigations in these matters."

Goldberg smiled and nodded, "Speaking for the Company, I feel comfortable with you assuming a command role. However, please let us thank Agent Stone and his colleagues for their excellent work so far. I think it would be to our advantage for Agent Stone to continue working on the case with you, as I'm sure he has already gathered considerable information that may be of help."

Dixon spoke grudgingly, "Stone, I think maybe I was a little hasty in my assessment. Perhaps you would care to brief me about what you have uncovered so far." Stone looked from one man to the other, "That's fine with me sir. Another professional on the job will be most welcome." Stone smiled at Dixon. "Maybe, sir, we can continue our investigations tomorrow morning which will give me time to collate the evidence so far accrued?"

Dixon nodded, "Well gentlemen and lady, until tomorrow then." Stone headed for the door followed by Susan and Fisher. "Not you Chief Fisher," said the Manager, "We still need you to provide a Company brief on Base security issues." Fisher stopped, looked at Stone and shrugged, "See you later." Stone closed the office door and leaned against the opposite wall. "Well, Sue, this changes everything. We have a late night ahead of us." He straightened up and started to walk towards the canteen, "Coffee first I think." Susan placed her hand on his shoulder, "Do you trust that bastard Sloane?"

"At the moment, Honey, I don't trust anyone," Stone answered. Then checked himself and smiled, "Except you, of course," "That's nice," she said. "Be careful with Dixon though, I have an uneasy feeling about that one."

Sitting down with their coffee, both Susan and Stone pulled out their hand computers comparing notes. Suddenly Stone looked up, "I think I will need to interview the Flight Controller, I missed out on an interview with him on my last trip, he was on Earth at that time. I have a feeling that he may be able fill in some blank spaces." "I'm almost sure that I have a general picture of what's going on, but I don't see a motive for it yet. Why would the LPS damage a reactor, but not incapacitate it? I can understand them destroying the Shuttles. That had the effect of interfering with the company's profits but surely permanently taking the reactor out of service would have a greater long term effect? It doesn't make sense. Finish your coffee and let's go and talk with the Flight Controller, what's his name?" Susan consulted her computer, "Rowland, Phillip he's been with the Company for ten years." Stone stood up, draining the last of his coffee. "Ok, let's go see what Mr Rowland has to say."

Leaving the canteen they walked towards the Control Centre. As they approached the general Shopping Mall, they noticed five men approaching from the opposite direction. As they walked past some sixth sense made Susan turn to look back. For Susan, everything slowed down. She saw the leading man swinging a fire axe at her head. She easily ducked under the blow at the same time flicking her open palm between the man's legs and slapping his groin area with her open palm, fingers flicking up into the man's scrotum. The man shrieked and collapsed onto the ground. As he was falling a second man ran forward a short bladed knife held low. She twisted to one side letting the knife pass her at waist height and drove her elbow into the man's throat. He fell gasping for air and clutching his ruined larynx. The third man had tackled Stone who had turned at the first sign of trouble. However, his assailant had managed to land a blow to his left eye. He saw stars and briefly his vision went black. Quickly recovering, Stone managed to land a heavy blow to the man's stomach and stepping back brought his foot up between the man's legs. The last two men saw what had happened and after a brief pause, turned and fled. But Susan was not to be cheated. Reaching forward at incredible speed she managed to catch the collar of the slower of the two and with a quick backward jerk brought him down so that the back of his head slammed into the ground with a violent thud. Susan was not finished, the anger in her had risen to almost fever pitch. She grabbed her first assailant round the neck in a strangle hold and applied a sideways twist. Then she spoke in a low growl. "I have but to move my arm just one centimetre and then your neck snaps. The only chance you have is to tell me who sent you." The man smiled, "If I told you then I'd be dead inside one hour, so I'll take my chance with you." There was a crunching sound and the man went limp. She spun round and caught the second man round the neck, "Now are you prepared to take a chance on me also?" she said applying a little more pressure until the neck started to creak. The man struggled briefly, then slumping down croaked, "Ok, Ok. We got an E-message telling us that you were a threat and to make sure you did not continue to stick your nose where it wasn't wanted." "Did that include killing us?" Susan growled. "We thought so," the man answered. "Who do you work for on the Base?" "Maintenance and mining, both." "And this extra kind of work, who employs you to remove people?" "Occasionally we get foreigners from off-planet who sometimes can cause trouble for the regulars who live here. We adjust their attitude, on request." "And this job?" said Susan applying a little more pressure. "We don't know, but it has to be someone high up with money. We aren't cheap." "How much for this job?" "One million Credits between us," came the answer. Susan released the man and noticed that Stone had not moved from his last position. He just stood and gazed at his wife in awe. "Remind me never to argue with you in future." She smiled sweetly, "I couldn't hurt you, Honey anyway, what you want to do with this lot?" Stone thought for a moment, then tapped a number on his wristband to call Fisher. He spoke into the air, the bone conduction device behind his ear buzzed then Fisher answered "Fisher here." "Hi, Karl, things are warming up a little, I have some customers for you." The voice vibrating behind his ear sounded tinny, "What gives Stone?" "Some people tried to mess with my lady and are now in need of Medical Services and later a warm cell." "Ok, where are you?" "Just outside the Company supermarket in the domestic area." "Right, I'll send a couple of the lads to pick them up. Anything else?" "No we are on our way to see Philip Rowland at Control Central. Maybe you would like to swing by our room later, we have many things to talk about." "Ok, see you then."

After Fisher's men had arrived and taken charge of the injured men Susan and Stone headed for the Control Centre. Rowland was not at his workstation when they arrived and they were told that he had been called away but would be back shortly. After ten minutes Rowland appeared. As he entered the room he saw Stone and Susan sitting on a bench-seat next to his console. He looked startled to see them there. Then with an obvious effort he relaxed and smiled. "Agent and Mrs Stone I believe. What can I do for you?" "You can cut the crap for a start," Susan replied. "I'm guessing, but I don't think you expected to see us. Am I right?" Rowland looked confused, "I don't know what you are talking about. I've just returned from the Manager's office talking to a CIS guy about what happened with the Shuttles. He tells me that he's heading the investigation and that you are working for him, right?" Stone waited a few seconds before answering, "Actually I work for a different section of CIS. However, that should not concern you. You just need to understand that you are compelled under Senate legislation to answer my questions." Rowland shrugged, "If I can help you I will." "What do you know of an organisation called the LPS?" "Nothing. I've heard of them of course, as has everyone on the Base, but beyond the fact that they have made some vague threats, nothing."

"Where were you when the second shuttle incident occurred?"

"I was in the Command Centre with Max, discussing the schedule for the next launch. Why?" "So you did not hear the order given to the shuttle computer by the pilot to launch the Shuttle?" "No, but I know she did. All operations are recoded automatically and I have listened to that recording several times. There is no doubt that she gave those launch orders,"

"Would it surprise you to know that the orders given came not from the Pilot but from a recording inserted into the Shuttle PA system?" Rowland looked startled,

"Impossible! For the voice operated launch sequence to work, someone had to deliberately activate the launch computer. Why would anyone do that?" "Exactly... Why? I have to say, that you should consider your next answer carefully. On the first Shuttle accident, who was responsible for checking the GO sequence for the Launch computers?"

"That would be engineering. They have the final say on launch safety. I, as the Flight Controller, have the final say to go or not, but I act upon engineering's launch advice."

"And that would be Max, yes?" "I guess so, but he would only act when he had received confirmation from all his various sections."

"I assume that all the telemetry from the launches are readily available and indeed there must be some sort of interim findings based on that telemetry?"

"The telemetry for the first accident has been sent to Earth for analysis, and the initial report indicated that there were simultaneous program malfunctions on three of the Shuttle's flight computers. These lasted for about one second, before the programs were automatically reset. The computers then re-commenced acceleration. Unfortunately this occurred at a critical point in the launch and the first mistiming was sufficient to place a powerful magnetic drag on the Shuttle that slowed it significantly. After the computers restarted they attempted to increase acceleration to reach launch velocity. Sadly the restart came too late and the Shuttle failed to reach its terminal launch speed … End."

Rowland spread his hands outward in a hopeless gesture and shook his head.

Stone pondered his next question carefully, "Have there ever been simultaneous program failures in the past?."

"A good question. I don't know if it was a program failure. Certainly it could not be a power failure; all systems are run with battery back-up."

"Three computers issue commands together and at least two computers must agree. It is possible that it may have been a system failure rather than program failure. Any abnormality in external systems allows the two monitoring computers to override instructions and bring the system back on line, within strict parameters." Can you think of anything that would cause a hardware malfunction in all three computers?" "Most unlikely; the only possibility was that the system detected an abnormality in the rate of acceleration too late in the launch sequence and attempted to correct at the last minute. That could only happen if there was a load mass discrepancy, but that's also most unlikely. Launch weight is checked by three different departments on loading and the computers monitor the acceleration rate. A mass discrepancy would be detected well in advance, and the launch should have been aborted."

Stone stood up, "Would an increased mass of say, 70-80 kilograms make an appreciable difference to the launch acceleration rate?" Rowland nodded, "That would alter the pre-programmed firing rate of the linear motors, I would have to calculate the difference in acceleration," "Enough to kick in the failsafe computers?" asked Susan.

"Possibly," came the reply. "Again I will have to calculate the difference in acceleration rate." Stones eyes lit up. There it was again, the sudden intuitive leap that Miles had spoken about. But before he could voice his thoughts, Susan asked

"I know what you are thinking — what was the mass of our missing agent Eric Carlsen?" "So, would there be a record of his weight for load purposes? Every passenger on lunar flights is weighed to within a couple of grams." she turned to Rowland,

"Do you still retain the weight records for incoming passengers, say from about four months ago?"

"Of course," came the reply, "We keep all records for two years."

"Please look up the record for Eric Carlsen." She said

"Rowland turned to the main console and tapped a request and almost immediately, a response came back, *No record of Eric Carlsen, please check the spelling of the passenger's name.* "Interesting," said Stone, "Just try Carlsen," *"No Carlsen on record.*

"Time to get serious." said Stone, "We know Eric Carlsen arrived here four months ago. We know that because he was a CIS officer. Also, we know that the Base Manager knew of him, because she mentioned a maintenance worker who disappeared at about the time of the Shuttle crash. So how come your system does not know of his arrival?"

"I'm not sure. Perhaps there has been a glitch in the system, could be many things," said Rowland, shrugging his shoulders. "I'll get my maintenance technician to check on it."

Stone sat on the edge of the desk, "You are responsible for maintaining this system in a safe working order. I've a mind to charge you with criminal negligence … what do you think?"

"The Launch Control system is extraordinarily complex so how can

I possibly personally monitor every small defect? It's just not possible." Stone relaxed a little. "Ok, so who beside yourself has full access to the launch computers?"

"Just about all the system operators and program maintenance staff." said the Controller. "Right," said Stone crossing the room to Susan, "I may wish to continue this interview at a later time, so make sure you are available ..." He turned to Susan, "Let's go and talk to Max." ......

When they arrived at the Engineering Centre Max was talking to one of the launch technicians. He saw Susan and Stone and quickly broke of the conversation and hurried towards them. "Harry, Susan, What can I do for you?" Max was wearing a standard communications headset. He stopped, appeared to listen for a moment, then spoke into his headset. "Yes, clear the bloody landing site today. Don't argue!" He turned back to them, "Sorry about that," he said, "I have an unscheduled Shuttle landing due in tomorrow, and I have to clear the landing pad in a hurry. I wouldn't mind but it's not even a Company job." "If you're busy Max, we can come back later today." "No, that's fine. It's up to the field crew now." "Can we go to your office Max? There's a few points I need your help with." Max gestured to a door at one side of the Centre. They walked to the office. Max sat behind his desk and Susan and Stone sat on two chairs opposite the desk. Stone spoke first, giving the impression of slight confusion. "Max, I've just been interviewing your Flight Controller, Rowland. I have tried to put together the events leading up to the two Shuttle incidents. He tells me that on the initial analysis of the first incident indicates that it may have been caused by a computer program malfunction causing the monitoring computers to briefly reset the system. This in turn caused a short deceleration at a critical point in the launch sequence. What do you think?"

Max paused and put his palms together forming a steeple with his fingers. "I think that it would require some sort of common external stimulus for the programs in all three computers to fail simultaneously."

"A payload weight discrepancy, for instance?" said Susan mildly.

"Max looked at Susan with a surprised expression on his face, "Why would there be a weight discrepancy? Overall mass is checked at three separate stages of the loading, and just prior to launch." Stone interjected, "Even so … is it possible that this would cause some kind of problem?" "A whole lot a things would have to go wrong at the same time for that to happen," said the Engineer. "Firstly, the acceleration would need to be below launch limit due to excess load mass. At the start of the launch cycle, the computers would automatically either increase thrust or abort the take off. Each of the three launch computers issue directives to the accelerator and each computer casts a vote on the truth of each directive. If one computer disagrees with the votes of the other two, then then they may decide to abort and shut down the system. Or if the computers think the launch is still viable, they will instantly re-set their programs and the launch will continue. From an initial quick and dirty examination of the telemetry data it appears that this was precisely what happened."

"But why was it so late in the launch sequence before the computers voted to reset?" Susan asked, "I speak as an aerospace engineer now of course. It appears on the surface to be almost impossible that the three computers failed to detect an acceleration error early enough to adjust acceleration or abort the launch."

Max looked troubled, "We sent the telemetry data to the Nassau Space Centre for detailed analysis, but we're yet to receive a report from them."

Stone stood up and began pacing around the room, "Ok, Max, let's look at the second incident. Rowland says that the pilot issued a launch directive to the on-board computer. Is that true?" "Yes, we listened to the cockpit voice recorder after the incident." "What I'm about to tell you, Max, is known only to a few people. The voice heard giving the launch directive was not the pilot herself, but a recording from a previous launch." Max jumped to his feet. "What! Do you have anything that proves that?" Susan held up the chip she had found on the shuttle, "This," she said. "Where did you get that?" said Max.

"On the floor of the shuttle after I recovered the pilot. The Address System was wrecked and this must have fallen out." Max took the chip, looked at it closely and returned it to Susan.

"All right, suppose the order was issued by the PA system, it still requires someone to physically activate the Launch sequence computer, i.e. press a button as well as issue a verbal order. Why the hell would the pilot do that?"

Stone stopped his pacing, "Good question, and one I'm yet to find a solution to." He turned quickly to Max, changing the subject,

"What do you know of the reactor incident five months ago?"

"Apart from what everyone else knows, very little. There was a minor blow-out in one of the reactor coolant pipes. Fortunately it wasn't the main coolant feed, but still the pile scrammed and shut down auxiliary power for three days while repairs were made. I'm an aerospace engineer so if you want to know more you'll have to talk to Vlad Petrovic, he's the guy hired to maintain the reactor. Both of us will be glad when they replace the damn thing with a decent Fusion Reactor."

Stone remembered with interest his interview with this engineer. He wondered how Springfield was getting on with his Earth-side investigations.

"Thanks, Max. I'll let you get back to work, sorry to be a nuisance." Stone said as he and Susan rose to their feet. "No problem." replied the Engineer. "Maybe I'll see you later for a drink?" "That will be good, 'till later then." Stone and Susan let themselves out into the Central Engineering concourse and headed for the Security Chief's office.

CHAPTER 10

Fisher was not there when they arrived at his office, however his Sergeant was, guarding the prisoners in the holding cells. "When will the boss be back?" asked Stone. "Probably later today. He had to go and see the Company Vice President, who wanted a full report to go to his pet CIS guy. That's weird, because we've already briefed them on everything we know. I guess there's other stuff that's worrying them about this mess. Also it appears that some government people are arriving tomorrow. Nobody seems to know who they are or what they want, but you can bet it isn't anything good."

Susan and Stone waited for about twenty minutes and were just about to leave when a very angry Fisher appeared, fuming and muttering about incompetence and stupidity. Suddenly he smiled looking sheepishly then relaxed and took out his favourite bottle.

"Want some," he asked. "No thanks," replied Stone, "I need a clear head today."

"I'll have one," said Susan making a face at Stone. Stone shrugged, "I guess I could use one too. What did the evil trio want?" Fisher swallowed a hearty drink, relaxed and recited the gist of the meeting. They had wanted an assurance that anything Fisher discovered was to be reported directly to the Manager. They also wanted to know about the three guys in custody, suggesting that they should be released into the custody of the Chief Superintendent.

"I hope you told them that that wasn't going to happen?" said Stone.

"As a matter of fact, I'm not sure if I still have a job with the

Company. I was most insistent on keeping the prisoners in close custody and in my care. The CIS guy wanted to know about the dead man and who killed him. It told them that during the struggle he fell and broke his neck, and that nobody was to blame, just an accident. I can tell you that they were not happy with that one, muttering stuff about damage to the Company's image, etc." He took another drink, "Anyway here they stay until released into Federal custody, Oh yes! They told me that some Federal types were coming in tomorrow and if I valued my career with the Company I would be careful about making wild and unsubstantiated comments that may indirectly interfere with the operation of the Base… Ho-Hum …"

Stone digested this information for a few minutes while Susan and Fisher exchanged pleasantries. Then he asked.

"What do you know about Vlad Petrovic?" "Just that he's our Nuclear Specialist and looks after the power plant. He's a pretty quiet guy, never in trouble." "Was he interviewed after the reactor accident?"

"I wanted to, but the Manager said the reactor accident was an administrative and technical matter and that there was little to interest the security section. I know better than to argue. However, it is interesting to note the accident happened on the same date that the maintenance guy had his heart attack — I guess I better not make wild and unsubstantiated assumptions though." he finished his drink and asked. "Anything new from the Controller?" Stone thought of telling his friend about his theory on the cause of the Shuttle incidents, but decided that the fewer people who knew about it the better. "Very little. They think that it was a computer glitch that caused the first shuttle crash, but they are waiting for a detailed analysis from Earth. Oh, by the way, some information may be coming in about our missing maintenance man. Let me know if you hear anything." "Ok, Harry will do." Stone was very weary when he left the Security Office.

Contrary to belief, low gravity can be more tiring than Earth standard. However Stone's tiredness was due to frustration and of course the fight with the would-be assassins. Susan was asleep almost as soon as her head touched the pillow. Stone's mind however would not let go of the problem. The solution to everything was almost tangible, but frustratingly would not clarify in his mind. He drifted off to sleep thinking about the day's interviews, something was not quite right ... something........

He woke early the next day period, still thinking about the interviews. What was it that Max had said that was a little odd? Susan had just woken and smiled at her husband, "Morning, Honey, is there is such a thing here as a shower?" Stone smiled back, "Together?" The time limit on the shower was just enough to soap up and rinse off so they decided to dispense with the soap and use the extra time to better advantage. Afterwards, as Stone was towelling his wife dry he marvelled at her perfect body, tracing her spine with his fingers, down to the cleft of her buttocks. "No," he thought, "Work to do." Gathering all his willpower, he turned her to face him and kissed first her eye-lids then her lips. She responded once again to his touch. He smiled, "Time for breakfast, don't you think?" she smiled coyly back at him, "I thought you had already had breakfast?" Pushing her away firmly, he finished drying himself and put on a clean jumpsuit, "Let's go, we have a shuttle to meet."

The canteen was unusually full for that time of day, and Stone realised that the arrival of an unscheduled shuttle would raise interest in the normally dull lives of many on the Base. Filling up on local grown cereal, they decided to splash out on eggs at huge expense. The limited supply of eggs came from a chicken farm hatchery in the hydroponics wing of the Base at 100 credits per egg, the same cost as his hotel room on Gamma 5. "What the hell," said Stone, "The Company will pay."

After breakfast they headed for the Arrivals Concourse. The Shuttle was not due to arrive for another thirty minutes, so Stone took time to review his notes. His computer, while it had repaired itself, was still defective and missing some critical data. He guessed he would have to manually add data from what he could remember.

Sitting down on a coloured plastic bench, he started to go over the data that he had lost. Mathew still had not regained his personality and Stone wondered if it ever would. "Mathew, print out all data relevant to my last 'Guess' interviews." The voice sounding in his ear was obviously mechanical in nature but some of the old Mathew still shone through.

A steady pseudo-paper strip issued from the little computer. This strip was manufactured inside the machine by an electro-thermal chemical reaction. Stone wondered if he had enough print liquid left, he could not remember when he last filled the machine. He started examining the strip for possible clues linking his last interviews with this current investigation. Paul Miles, when he had said that Stone probably had some of the answers, had not reckoned with the partial destruction of Mathew's memory or the loss of the first print-out. But he was sure that he could reconstruct much of the data from memory. The first name to appear was the Russian Vlad Petrovic. Several of the answers were hesitant and obviously fabrications. "Perhaps Petrovic could be a good starting point." He thought.

Just then the Public address system cracked into life.

The shuttle g575 is about to land, please remain seated and do not approach the security desk until all passengers have disembarked.

Stone stopped the printout and pocketed his computer. The only indication of the Shuttle's landing came from tremors transmitted through the floor, and a slight rattle from the metal walls of the Arrivals Bay. Just then Stone noticed that the Manager was waiting by the reception desk. Stone turned to Susan, "Maybe we should come back later," he said, nodding towards the reception committee. Susan nodded in agreement, and hooking his arm in hers, she led them back to the domestic area.

After about ten minutes there was a loud hiss as the hatches of the Shuttle and Arrival Bay equalised pressure. Then the Main Concourse hatch swung open. The Manager's reception committee was waiting at the hatch doorway. Two men walked through into the Arrival Bay, Pearson stepped forward. "Welcome to Armstrong, Mr ... er. Sorry, your staff did not provide your names on the manifest."

"Gibson, the shorter of the two answered, and this is Faulding, my assistant."

"We were messaged to expect a visit from Senate representatives, and to provide assistance. So on behalf of the Company, if I can be of any service, you only need to ask"

"Thank you, Miss Pearson is it?" Pearson nodded. "We have been commissioned by the Senate to carry out a fact finding mission relating to the annual cost of launch operations. As you are aware, the Senate pays a considerable annual sum to your Company for supporting the Federal Space program." Pearson smiled. "Perhaps we can continue this discussion in my office, after you have rested." She smiled again and gestured towards the security desk and reception area. "If you will follow me, sir we will get you settled in the executive accommodation." The small man gave her a beaming smile, "That is most kind of you, Rosemary, I may call you Rosemary?" Pearson was a little surprised at the familiarity, but the man seemed pleasant enough. "Glad to help … And yes you may call me Rosemary." For some reason, this man put the Manager at ease, relaxed even, something she had not felt for many months,

The two collected their card-keys and gave their bags to the two waiting assistants.

"I will see you to your rooms, then if you don't mind we can meet later, after you have refreshed."

"That is just perfect," the small man replied." Say in about four hours in your office, if that is acceptable?" "I will look forward to that." Pearson turned to her two assistants, "Let's go. Lead the way, Michael." The two assistants set off down the long tunnel towards the domestic area, followed by the Manager and her guests.

From some distance away Stone looked in amazement at the two new arrivals. He gestured to Susan and they followed the group at a safe distance to the executive accommodation where they stopped at two adjacent rooms. The shorter man shook hands with Pearson, who turned and left for the administration area. Waiting until the corridor was clear, Susan and Stone approached. Stone knocked on the first of the two doors. The door opened, revealing the short man and a beaming smile. He stepped forward towards Susan and kissed her hand. There was only one person that could do that and live, 'Paul!' The other door opened, and the second man stood looking at Stone with a grin.

"Hello, Harry. I'll bet didn't expect to see me?" said Miles, grasping Stone's hand.

"By all the gods, no!" said Stone. Then his gaze traced a path towards the other man,

"Good to see you too Springfield, very happy to see you. We definitely can use your talents." Stone looked at Miles with disbelief. "How did you manage to get here? Last we heard was that some bastard had grabbed you." Miles waved his hand dismissively.

"You don't think I left anything to chance do you? You know me better than that. I left a message with Stevens at the Ottawa Office. Instructions were simple, find me and get me out. Stevens is a very fine fellow. With the information you gave him and my message, he managed to trace me through the security cameras. Never did like the intrusive things, but this time they proved useful. That was five days ago. Some bastard tried to put me through a mind wringer, but either there was not enough mind to work with, or it was total incompetence on the part of the doctor. We will never know — Stevens arranged for him to disappear permanently." He relaxed a little, "It took a couple of days for my personal mind-bender to fix me to a reasonable level, then I headed for Gamma 5 expecting to see you. Instead, I met 'Springthing' or whatever his real name is and he briefed me on some very interesting stuff he'd got from interviewing the families from the list provided by Stevens." Rubbing his hands together, "Now, I need a coffee — not plastic crap, real coffee. Then we should find a secure area to talk."

Nobody was aware of the man watching them on a surveillance monitor, and as they headed to the canteen, he dialled a specific contact number into his communicator. "They've arrived!" he reported.

After Miles had finished his coffee, he turned to Springfield. "Maybe we should find that secure area that we were talking about on the way here. The Security office perhaps?" Stone interrupted, "Paul, before we go, maybe we should talk about what we should share with Company Security. We think Fisher's Ok, but what about the rest?" Miles stood up and shook his head, "A good point. Harry. Maybe we should not discuss what we have deduced so far, rather we should simply present the facts in evidence, yes?" "I would not present too much of that, either." Said

Stone. "Ok, just the bare facts for the Security guys. Is there anywhere else secure here?" "Not sure, I'll check." Stone stood and walked to the door, Susan and the rest followed.

Arriving at the Security Office, they found Fisher behind his desk. Brief introductions followed and when everyone was seated Miles opened the conversation. Springfield poured himself a coffee and stood behind Miles. Leaning back in his seat, Miles put his hands behind his neck. "First … please note that I'm not at all sure about this LPS group. They are not behaving like a typical evangelistic organisation. For instance, historically most groups of this type have not tried to hide their activities, but have advertised their intent to the world. This lot are not following this established pattern they are more secretive."

Stone nodded, it was a conclusion he had come to himself when he viewed his data, remembering the thoughts he had had on the Shuttle —It was almost as if they didn't exist.

Miles went on, "So I started to think … is this organisation for real?" He spread his hands expressively. "Sadly, there is such an organisation, but upon investigation, we found that none of its members had been to the Moon, nor did they have many supporters."

Stone agreed, "Paul, I came to the same conclusion. But I was side-tracked by the Shuttle crash and the Reactor incident although I did not immediately associate them directly with the LPS at first, because there was no mention in my initial brief for me to investigate possible sabotage on the Base. I assumed that a Field Agent would deal with that." Stone looked pointedly across the table at Miles, who shrugged and laughed, "I knew I could rely upon you to wake up sooner or later. What I wanted from you was a clean analysis of the employees working at Armstrong. As you had guessed, a Field Operative had already been despatched to cover possible LPS involvement." A look of deep concern spread over Miles' face. "Initially, the agent reported that he could find no evidence of LPS involvement. So imagine my chagrin when I received a broken interim report from our man, that there appeared to be a connection. It just didn't make sense."

Stone looked with annoyance at Miles, "Our man's Name was Eric Carlsen, and I've reason to believe that he is no longer with us."

"Sorry, Harry, I get caught up with the game rather than the players." Stone relented a little,

"You always were a cold-hearted bastard Paul, but I forgive you because you get results. Just make sure that you send a personal message to the man's family, and don't farm the job out to some bloody nondescript clerk." Miles smiled and nodded. "That's twice I've seen him smile today, maybe he is going soft." Stone muttered to himself.

Miles continued, "Anyway, I am now convinced that something else is driving all these incidents — and I do not believe in accidents."

Miles turned and spoke to Springfield, "I think it's time for you to tell them what you uncovered on your last visit to Earth. And start at the beginning."

Springfield looked over his cup at Stone, "You know we asked Stevens to get us information on the people on your list. Well, Stevens went a lot further. There were some huge gaps in your data, not surprisingly after the sabotage to your computer. Anyway Stevens, as promised, delivered the information requested. But before I met the courier, I intercepted a CIS agent who was detailed to follow me. Strange, only Stevens and I knew where I was to meet his courier. I can only assume that there is a rotten agent somewhere in the system who has access to Stevens' office. Anyway the most important thing I discovered is that all the families on the list were under threat of harm. They are now relocated to a safe area." Stone looked up, "If Stevens' office has been penetrated, what's to guarantee the safety of these people?" "I personally organised the relocation using civilian police. Not even Stevens knows where they are, I'm the only guy who knows their whereabouts except the two police who helped with the move and are maintaining a watch."

"Good, that means it's safe to talk with a few people ..." Stone leaned closer to Miles and whispered, "Starting with Mr Petrovic. Let's err on the side of safety and not advertise who we talk with, agreed?" Miles nodded.

Stone told Miles about the recording chip that Susan had found on the shuttle and their conclusion that this was a case of sabotage and murder. Miles thought for a moment, "Perhaps we should talk to the others on our list before we talk with our illustrious guests. I'm surprised that they did not come to the arrivals hall to greet us. We did send a message that some high ranking government officials were coming on a fact-finding mission, and requested assistance from the Base Management and that a low profile was to be maintained. By the way our names are now Gibson and Faulding, I'm Gibson."

Miles looked worried, "Maybe we don't rate or they don't care, the last hypothesis concerns me more. You do realise that the Manager's mother is one of the people under our protection.

The picture that we are painting here is a simple one of standover tactics to hide something, but what? What can be so important as to warrant the involvement of so many people, and why sabotage the Shuttles?

Stone cut in, "I'm guessing that the second shuttle accident was to silence the pilot, but what could she possibly know that would necessitate the destruction of yet another Shuttle?"

Miles looked a little furtive and smiled, "Maybe the first accident was just that, an accident or miscalculation of some sort. After what you said, Harry I believe that it was probably unintentional. So assuming that there was a load error of some sort, how did that error get past so many routine but very precise checks? There has to be interference of some sort to negate early error detection, but why do it, anyway?"

Stone looked at Springfield, "Charlie, give me that list you got from Stevens,"

He took the list and mentally ticked off each of the names in turn, then he looked up and smiled. "You do realise that all of the names on this list with the exception of Petrovic, are related in some way with either launch, cargo or load control. The odd man out is Petrovic, so perhaps we should talk with him next. With your permission, Miles I'd like to tackle this one, with Susan. Perhaps you, Springfield and Fisher can tackle the others. But first I would let them know their families are safe in protective custody, which may help them relax." Stone stood up. "I am particularly interested in Load Controller Haslop, in Lim Lee the Miner and in Arnold Mason the programmer. Lim Lee is another odd one out, but I think he may be a key player. Maybe we should meet back here later this day period say ... 17:00 local time." With that He and Susan left the office and headed for the Reactor bay." "You are going let to me help aren't you?" Said Susan.

After getting lost a couple of times Susan and Stone finally located the Nuclear Engineer's workshop. They had expected it to be near the Reactor space. However it was down a passage that ran off the main Engineering Concourse.

Initially Petrovic was reluctant to talk, stating that Stone had already interviewed him at length and he could add little to what he had already said. However when asked about the Reactor incident he became positively opposed to speaking further.

Stone sat on the bench opposite the engineer, and in a quiet voice began the interview. "Firstly, what can I call you ... Vlad?"

Petrovic shrugged his shoulders, and speaking in fluent English with no trace of accent, replied, "Call me what you like, I'm still not required to talk to you about Company business."

Susan squatted next to the workbench, "Ah, but you are, Mr. Petrovic!" she said.

Petrovic looked from one to the other, "What can you do to me ... lock me up? Ha! That would be good. Look ... the Base Manager has warned me not to speak to you because there is a more senior CIS agent on the Base at the moment, who, she says, is running this enquiry, and if I speak to others it may compromise his investigation. So you see I don't have to talk to you at all... Now if you don't mind ...."

"Ah, but I do mind," countered Stone, "I mind very much. I am appointed and empowered by the World Senate to look into matters that may involve an illegal organisation and possible sabotage to

Earth-owned assets. In fact, the Green Office is partially funding this investigation. So let's cut the crap and start to be cooperative, or I will place you into custody for obstruction of an officer in the course of his duty. Clear!"

Petrovic, went pale and staggered a little.

Susan moved forward and grabbed him as he was about to fall. She helped him to a chair and looked at her husband. "Nice one, Harry." She undid the top fastener on Petrovic's jump suit. "Honey, can I ask a couple of questions?" she said.

Stone looked amused, "Sure. Maybe I was a little heavy handed. Sorry, Vlad, but this business is very frustrating."

Susan squatted in front of the badly shaken man. "Vlad, I can call you Vlad … yes?" The engineer nodded. "Good … Vlad, we do know that you are married with three children, but when interviewed by my colleague here you stated that you were not married and indeed in no form of contractual obligation at all, now why did you say that?"

Petrovic, bent his head, put his face in the palms of his hands and seemed about to burst into tears, his shoulders shaking. "They said if I spoke about the plant incident to anyone my family would suffer. Now you force me to talk with you. They will know already you are here. My family is now in danger, and so are you!"

"I can assure you, Vlad," said Susan, "your family is safe. Our agents have already recovered your young son and daughter and they are in a safe place, and no-one can hurt them now. In fact, your whole family has been relocated."

"You don't know who you are dealing with. They have spies everywhere, in the police, the CIS and the Company. No person is safe."

Susan placed her hand on his shoulder, "The only people who know your family's whereabouts are me, my partner, and three other agents who are part of this investigation."

"What about the Manager and the bigshots from the Company?"

"They know nothing." replied Susan. "Look, just a few simple questions, then we will re-unite you with your family, Ok?"

The man relaxed and sighed, "Ok, ask away. You are sure they're safe … aren't you?"

"Yes, I guarantee they are safe. Now, the first question is ... What happened to the reactor coolant system?"

The man sat up and straightened his shoulders, "I inspected the whole of the reactor system carefully that morning, that is, the morning when the reactor scrammed. After I finished my inspection I checked all the temperature and power output readings. All was good, so I returned to my workshop and was writing my report when the monitoring system, over there," he pointed to a large control console, "lit up like an old-fashioned Christmas tree, and the shutdown alert sounded."

He reached for a tissue and wiped his brow. "Then the Manager called me and said that I was needed in the Reactor space. Not knowing what the problem was, I put on my radiation suit and went to the Reactor chamber. I found the whole room full of steam, and the radiation counters screaming. I noticed a small hole in one of the subsidiary coolant pipes. I immediately grabbed an emergency patch and slapped it over the hole. Then I voided all the air out onto the lunar surface.

After about ten minutes I checked that the patch was holding, and re-pressurised the chamber." A couple of days later, when the secondary radiation level had dropped to a manageable level and the pressure in the coolant pipe had dropped to zero, I was able to get general engineering to weld a sleeve around the pipe making it far stronger than it was before."

Susan rocked back on her heels, "What do you think caused the leak?"

"I know what caused the leak. There was a small piece of an electronic mechanism on the floor of the room, and it had not been there that morning. I am, after all, a good engineer, and I recognised the device as part of a digital timer. You don't have to be a rocket scientist to work out the rest."

"So what you are saying is, someone caused the damage deliberately ... yes?" The engineer nodded.

"Then what happened,"

Petrovic stood up, "Look, you really are sure my family is safe ...?"

"Yes. What did you do next?"

"I reported my suspicions to the Base Manager. She was really angry with me and told me not to be so melodramatic and stupid. I felt like an idiot, and thinking back felt that I had over-reacted. Anyway she told me not to spread unfounded rumours and to get back to work."

"And then?"

"That night I received a microwave video-message from my hometown in Russia. I could not see the face of the man who was speaking, but he showed me my family sitting together in a café, He told me to keep my mouth shut or something nasty will happen to them. But to make sure, he said that he would take my young son and daughter captive and keep them for three months. If I kept silent, they would be released.... That all I know ... Now please get me out of here!"

"One last question, Vlad Why do you think anyone would do this, It only shut the reactor down for three days, so no real damage was done to operations. So why do it?"

"But there were changes to operations," he replied. "A launch cannot take place without the reactor being in service. Although the solar panels alone can supply enough energy, the Launch Standard Operational Procedure requires all power supplies to be on-line and fully functional. So a launch was actually delayed by four days. It was merely a procedural delay, but a delay none-the- less, and it cost the Company a fair bit in delivery quota penalties."

Susan got up and helped the Engineer to his feet. "Thanks, Vlad. We want you to return to your quarters and lock yourself in. Don't open the door to anyone but us and don't speak to anyone. We are making arrangements for your return to Earth on the next Shuttle." The engineer looked miserable, but nodded.

After the Petrovic had left, Stone, turned to Susan. "I think this reactor incident was separate to the Shuttle incidents. It's possible that the reactor was sabotaged to deliberately delay a launch, but why? I think we need to hear what the Load Coordinator and the miner have to say. I'm now not at all convinced that there is a connection between the reactor incident and the Shuttle accident."

Susan nodded, "But first let's get some food, and then contact Miles to see he and Springfield have come up with."

CHAPTER 12

When Stone arrived at the Security Office ten minutes early Fisher and Springfield were already enjoying one of the Security Officer's special drinks, and Miles was seated behind the desk.

"Might have guessed," Stone remarked.

"This is space," said Springfield. "It's always after midday here."

Just then Susan came in, "I've been to check on Petrovic. He's settled down a little and is securely locked in his room. Karl, maybe you could organise a discreet guard on him?"

Fisher nodded, "I'll organise it now." He reached for his phone and spoke briefly…. "Done."

"What came of your interviews, and did you talk with Lee?" asked Stone. "We couldn't find Lee. They said he was working topside shift on a new mine site so I'll catch up with him later. I did talk to Haslop the Load Controller. His story is much as we expected. He was asked to modify the load weight for the first shuttle. Something to do with an undisclosed cargo. However he did say the calculations for overall weight were adjusted by an Arnold Mason. When I spoke to Mason via Sat-Link, he told me that he had been directed to reconfigure the program sequence for acceleration to take care of any discrepancies in payload, effectively hiding undisclosed cargoes."

Springfield adjusted his huge bulk in the chair. "Both men were relieved that their families were safe and Haslop wanted to go Earth-side as soon as possible."

Fisher looked from one to the other. "That's all very, well but what does it all mean?"

Stone sat and looked at Susan. "Maybe we should tell them what we think the reasoning was behind the Reactor sabotage?"

Susan described the interview with Petrovic, and their conclusion that the whole incident may have been to delay a shuttle launch, adding that there was still no apparent reason for arranging the delay.

"Maybe it's time for one final interview. When did you say Lee was returning?" asked Stone

Fisher spoke first, "He should be back by now, I'll check with his supervisor." Fisher tapped out a number on his wrist band and spoke into the air. "Mike, when does Lee get in from top-side?" Fisher looked puzzled. "That's strange … we were told he was working a shift in the new mine-site today. Any idea where we can find him then? Thanks, I'll send one of my boys out to find him, thanks, Mike."

Fisher turned to Stone. "His supervisor says that he was not on a scheduled shift today, but he apparently wanted to go top-side to get some ore samples. He should be back now. Mike suggested that he may be in the Minerals Laboratory."

Picking up his communicator, Fisher called his sergeant. "Alan … Chief here, go to the Minerals Lab and bring in Mining Technician Lee. By the way anything on our lady-friend yet? Ok, tell me when you get here."

Stone took out his computer and called up his latest list, then smiled. "I wonder, what could be so interesting to Lee that he goes to work on his day off?"

Miles who had been sitting quietly while all this took place, suddenly stood up and as the door opened. "Perhaps we should ask Mr Lee, this is probably him now."

But it wasn't Lee at all. It was a very worried-looking Base Manager. She stood in the doorway taking in scene before her. "I had word that you had begun your fact finding tour already. I thought we had an agreement that we would meet in my office and I would provide you with assistance…"

Miles stepped forward and extended his hand in greeting. "Ah,

Rosemary, how good of you to make the effort to look us up. Yes, as you can see, we have already begun our fact finding inquiries — I just didn't want to bother you at this early stage. However, I'm glad you're here now. We have an interesting little problem associated with the cost of payloads billed to the government."

Miles smiled and gestured to an empty seat. "You see, although we told you that the basis of our mission was to evaluate cost of operations, I can hardly be asked to ignore the last two incidents involving shuttle accidents … I'm sure my *masters* will want assurances for the safety of our personnel travelling on your system, and the last two incidents have caused us some concern.."

Miles sat opposite the Manager and took her hands in his. "I don't want to alarm you. But you see, although we are government officers our department is more concerned with possible terrorist activity rather than finance. I want you to know, that we are aware of the situation that you find yourself in, and we can happily assure you that your family has been safely placed in protective custody."

Pearson started to get up with a real look of fear on her face. Miles held onto her hand, and eased her back down.

Tears welled in the Managers eyes. "My family cannot be safe. You see I've been told that should I talk with anyone, my mother will be killed."

"Rosemary, that will not happen now, we are aware that you and several others on this Base are under threat, but I'm guessing that you do not know who is organising this whole thing or why they are doing it, therefore you cannot trust anyone. But I can assure you that your mother and family are safe."

The manager bowed her head and tears dripped onto her lap. "Thank God that's over," she said. "I've been frantic with worry for the last four months."

Miles patted her hands and sat back. "Now Rosemary, tell me exactly how you became involved with this?"

She sat up and wiped her eyes. "About four months ago I received a tele-message from my mother telling me that she had been threatened and that if I did not do what I was told, she would be killed. My mother is not a strong woman and was almost frantic. She begged me to cooperate. The next day I received a message on my personal console that something would take place and I was to ensure that the matter was dealt with as a routine enquiry. The rest of the details would be handled by other people."

She sniffed and continued. "Anyway, the next day we had a reactor incident followed by the disappearance of Eric Carlsen the maintenance worker. The doctor reported that he had suffered a heart attack. I realised that Graham's death may not have been natural causes. However I was worried about my mother, so I smoothed over the inquiry as best I could" She looked at Fisher, "Sorry, Karl." Fisher nodded back.

Miles smiled and patted her hands again. "Now then Rosemary, tell me about the Company executive and the police officer who are currently on the base.

"Like you, they were supposed to be on a fact-finding mission about the shuttle incidents. The Company man is the Vice President of Transglobal, Alan Goldberg and the other was introduced as Chief Superintendent Henry Dixon an officer of the Criminal Investigation Service. I was interviewed by them first then they informed me that they would take over the accident investigations on behalf of CIS and Transglobal. They seemed particularly interested in Mr Stone's enquiries and the results produced by our Company Security Officer. Of course I was worried that they would investigate me and my part in the maintenance workers disappearance and also the death of Mark Graham. But they seemed more interested in protecting the interests of the company, and continued to play down anything that might harm the Company's reputation. I thought that this was a little strange for a CIS officer. However he may have been acting on instructions from the Senate. I wasn't sure, so I cooperated. Sorry, Mr Stone, but under the circumstances I had no choice."

Stone nodded at the troubled manager.

Miles broke in, "That's Ok, Miss Pearson I understand. If I may interrupt a little, could you please arrange for Goldberg and Dixon to be kept out of our way until we are ready to talk to them? And also to maintain the slight deception about our identities, for the moment at least." She nodded in agreement.

Miles stood up and took her by the arm and gently led her to the door. "Thank you for your help Rosemary. Perhaps we can continue our talk at a later time?" She meekly allowed herself to be ushered out of the room.

When she had gone Stone turned to Fisher, "I wonder what is keeping your Sergeant."

"I'll find out." replied Fisher.

Just then, the door opened and Sergeant Gregory appeared with a tall well-built man of Chinese appearance. The man looked anything but happy. Stone stepped forward extending his hand. "I take it you are Mr Lim Lee?" he said, shaking Lims's hand

"I am, and you are?" said Lim

"My name is Harry Stone, and this is my partner Susan and the other two gentlemen are Paul Gibson and Charles Fielding. Of course you know the Company Security Chief, Karl Fisher." Lee looked at each one and his shoulders seemed to slump.

Fisher turned to his sergeant, "Thanks Bil, I'll handle it from here." The sergeant nodded and left.

"Mr. Lim, please take a seat." said Stone using the Chinese form of address. Lim sat, looked down and waited.

"Now, Lim. Please don't be alarmed — everybody here is aware of your particular problem regarding your family."

Lim looked up, startled. "Who told you that I have a problem?"

"Lim you are not the only person who has this problem. We have already investigated several other workers who have had their families threatened. My colleague here has already interviewed your family in Kuala Lumpur, and I can assure you that they are no longer in danger. They have been relocated to a secure location known only to Mr. Fielding and no other, not even me."

Lee looked up at Stone, attempting to gauge the truth of it. He relaxed and said, "How can I help you?"

"My first question is … What are you expected to do, to guarantee the safety of your family?"

Lee looked wary. "Nothing really, I was just asked to go to the new mine, pick up a sealed packet and deliver it to the Load Controller at the launch site. I had to do that before each scheduled launch, without raising a formal load declaration."

"Do you know what was in the packet?"

"No I was told not to open the package under any circumstance, and that after one year I would be free to return home to my family."

"When were you first approached?"

"About five months ago I delivered the first sealed package. After that, I collected one package per week from the mine and took it to the Shuttle. Except for one week when the reactor broke down and the Shuttle could not launch. They never asked me to collect the package that week. Then just after the reactor was repaired, they told me to bring another two packages, but these were heavier."

"Who was the Load Controller you delivered the package to?"

"His name was Maurice Haslop."

"Ok, what is the main product from this new mine?"

"Helium - 3 and some rare earths, but mostly Helium – 3"

"When are you due to make another delivery?"

"Just before the next Shuttle which I understand is next week sometime, depending upon the repairs to the launch rail."

"My partner and I would like to visit this mine. Can you show me where you pick up the package?"

"I could if I wanted to end up like that nosy maintenance man who disappeared."

"What do you know about that?"

"Only that he was forever asking questions, and one day he was never seen again. Word has it that he must have really annoyed someone with his questions and he got the chop."

"Nobody thought to question his disappearance?"

"Yes. But the Base Manager said that she would handle it herself and she ordered a surface search. Then, after one week she gave up and filed a 'missing persons report' to the Company."

"The report indicated that the man may have strayed or had an accident on the surface and died. Anyway, if he was on the surface for one week it's was very unlikely that he would be still alive."

Fisher came from behind his desk, "When did you last see him?"

"Oh, about two Earth days before, he was talking to Max, the Flight Engineer."

"Ok, thanks Lim, we will be in touch. In the meantime this conversation never happened and you are to continue to collect packages as per normal."

Fisher placed his hand on Lim's shoulder, "If anything out of the ordinary happens, you are to tell me straight away, Don't Wait!"

"Yes of course." said Lim

Stone stood up and shook hands with the miner, "Thanks for your help, we will be in touch."

After Lim had left, Miles beckoned to Springfield and Fisher. "I need you two to go and have a talk with Haslop and get his side of the story." He turned to Stone. "Can you and Susan check out this mine site?"

Stone nodded. "Karl what's the name of the Mining Manager?" "Mike Simmons." Replied Fisher

. "Right," said Stone "Susan, let's pay Mr Simmons a visit."

CHAPTER 13

The Mining office was situated at the end of a long tunnel leading to the mineral processing plant and the loading bay where the minerals were brought in from the various mine sites. The Mining Manager rose from behind his desk as Susan and Stone entered.

Stone extended his hand in greeting. "Mr Simmons?"

"Yes that's right, and you must be the CIS people everyone is talking about."

"Correct, I'm Harry Stone and this is Susan my partner." Simmons shook hands first with Stone then with Susan. "How can I help?"

Stone explained that they wished to look at the new mine site to get a better feel for the mining process and asked if the Manager see his way clear to provide a guide and some transport.

"I'd love to help, but there are safety regulations that forbid people who are not vacuum-suit trained, to travel in Company transport on the surface..." Simmonds suddenly stopped and looked more closely at Susan. "I'm sorry. I remember you now from the shuttle incident a few days ago. You're the lady engineer that helped to rescue the pilot. My apologies that makes all the difference. I take it your partner has a working knowledge of vacuum procedures?"

"Of course. All CIS operatives undergo basic training in vacuum operations." She lied, smiling sweetly at the manager.

"In that case, I will drive you to the mine myself. Wait here a moment while I organise some suits." Simmons left the office.

"Lucky break," said Susan. Stone nodded in reply. Just then Simmons returned with two men carrying three vacuum suits.

"These should do the trick. Please note that the air-conditioning plants on these particular suits are guaranteed to operate for up to four hours, no more. That will limit our trip as it takes about thirty minutes to reach the site and thirty minutes to return. So, allowing for a one hour safety margin, we should aim to be back here in no more than three hours. Of course the tractor has its own air supply and conditioner which can keep three people going for about an extra five hours. After that, we would be in big trouble. Also note that the communicators on the suits are good for about ten kilometres, but work best in line of sight."

He held up a suit to Susan and gave another to Stone. Smiling he said, Do you need any help, Mr Stone?" Stone nodded and one of the men stepped forward and started to adjust the suit to fit.

After a final check on all three suits Simmonds led them down a long tunnel to an airlock that fed into the vehicle hangar bay. The bay was a vast cave-like structure. Inside this huge cavern stood many and various vehicles, from lifting cranes to large eight wheeled ten ton flatbed trucks with enclosed airtight cabins. At the far end of the bay stood three tractors each with eight balloon tyres. The tractors were built in two sections, a front driver's cabin with enough room for five people and a rear articulated cabin with seating for twelve. The rear cabin could be disconnected when not required. The electric motors driving the tractor were situated on the axle of each wheel and powered by large Photocell assisted power packs situated on the roof of each section.

The manager unhitched the rear section of the nearest tractor and climbed into the driver's seat. Stone and Susan sat in the back. Then Simmonds spoke softly into the communicator and a siren sounded in the bay. After a short while the inner hangar doors slid open leading into a smaller airlock chamber large enough to accommodate all three tractors and a single truck. The tractor rolled smoothly forward with just a faint whine of its motors. When the vehicle was inside the airlock chamber, the main hangar door closed, followed by a loud hiss as air was pumped into the main hangar bay. Then the outer airlock door slid open.

The tractor moved smoothly onto the dark lunar surface with only a slight whine vibrating through the hull. The landscape before them was dotted with large and small craters. The roadway leading away from the Base was lit by banks of high intensity LED lights. These lights not only lit the road surface but illuminated the cold, stark ground, casting sharply defined shadows at each uneven point on the surface.

The tractor picked up speed and headed down what appeared to be a brightly lit ribbon. The road wound round small mountains and craters for about thirty minutes before arriving at a vast quarry. The site was scattered with numerous sealed portable buildings, presumably miners' temporary accommodation. In the centre of the quarry stood a massive excavator loading a truck with ore. Figures in vacuum suits were busily going about their jobs. At the far end of the excavation stood the entrance to a deep mine shaft. The whole area was brilliantly illuminated, looking somewhat like a picture from Dante's Hell.

The tractor rolled to a stop at one of the larger buildings. Simmonds cycled the airlock on the vehicle and stepped onto the lunar surface.

His voice sounded over the suits' headsets. "Ok we're here," he said. "Follow me, but be careful of your suits."

They entered the building through a small airlock and when inside removed their helmets. Stone was surprised at the level of comfort that had been designed into the structure.

"Nice, yes?" said Simmonds with obvious pride. "Our miners are sometimes required to stay here on extended shifts, so we look to making life a little more relaxing for them."

The building consisted of six small rooms with a bed and private computer console in each. The main lounge area had comfortable seating and a dining table. There was a small galley-style kitchen off to one side of the main room. Near the entrance was a small room with hanging frames for vacuum suits. The only thing missing was washing facilities.

"Sorry no showers here — too hard to provide enough water. However on the other side of the compound is a sealed shower block with a water recycling system. Personally, I prefer to wait until I get back to Armstrong. It seems different there, somehow."

Susan wrinkled her nose at that comment, and Stone smiled at her reaction. She hadn't minded using recycled water in the showers on Gamma 5 and Armstrong, and he couldn't see what the difference was.

Stone removed his air conditioning pack and sat on one of the seats. "What is the main product from this mine site?"

"Helium-3," came the reply, "but of course some other rare earths and metals can be found in the deep-cut mine."

"Metals like what?" asked Stone

"Oh, some gold and platinum, not really worth our while mining. It's too heavy in payload costs to be commercially viable, but some miners are allowed to take small samples home with them as extra cargo. They have to pay the Company for the excess mass which can cost more than what the metal is worth, weight for weight."

"Things are usually pretty dull here during a working shift, except a few months ago when there was that business of the missing maintenance man. That caused a bit of excitement, I can tell you. Everyone was running around searching everywhere, didn't find him though. Probably fell down a deep shaft or something, I guess he will be found at some time or other."

Stone was acutely aware that the person referred to was their missing agent.

"What was he doing when he disappeared?" he asked.

"Not sure," came the reply. "He was supposed to be servicing one of our major drill rigs in the deep shaft. We looked there of course. He was a strange fellow, always asking questions, interested in everything, nice enough chap though."

"I'm interested in the engineering side of things," said Susan. "Can we go and look at the drill rig?"

"Sure," Simonds replied.

After replacing their helmets they cycled the airlock and headed towards the deep mineshaft.

When they reached it, Stone and Susan were surprised to be entering a slightly downward angled tunnel driven into the rock face instead of a deep shaft.

"Please be careful with your suits," said the manager. "We don't need any more accidents at this time."

The tunnel was about three metres wide and three metres tall, allowing all three to enter together. The inside of the tunnel was brightly lit by the same LED lighting as outside. Three miners were leaving the tunnel as they entered. They greeted the Manager with smiles. Popular guy, thought Stone.

Susan was studying the rock surface carefully as they moved down the tunnel. She stopped and took out a small hammer from her pack and tapped a couple of samples from the wall then put the hammer and samples into her pack.

Simonds looked amused, "No gold I'm afraid."

"No," she smiled, "but something more interesting maybe."

Continuing on down the tunnel they came across a couple of workers chipping away at the surface.

Susan stopped and looked more closely at what the men were doing. "Is that volcanic ash I see?"

One of the miners looked up and seeing Susan through the helmet smiled. "Yes, miss, pretty old stuff too. You have a good eye."

Susan thanked the man, then turned to the manager, "How far down does this tunnel go?"

"About three kilometre, we won't be able to go all the way down there today, there's not enough time, especially wearing these suits. In fact we should think about returning to the tractor soon, to stay within the safety limit."

"How do the miners work such long shifts then?"

"They have a different type of suit to the one you are wearing, plus they can replenish at one of the huts, but the replenishment packs don't match up with these older suits."

"I see, so where can we get hold of these special miners' suits?"

"They have to be made to order and specially fitted, unlike the general purpose suits we are wearing."

"In that case, can you arrange for a couple of suits to be made to fit us? The Senate will foot the bill?"

"Yes, I should be able to arrange that. I'll have to check with the equipment store, but it shouldn't be a problem."

"I suppose you have one already?" "Yes, but they are heavy and uncomfortable so I don't usually wear it on snap visits. These general purpose suits on the other hand are much easier to fit and wear."

"If you can arrange that then we'll come back out here tomorrow. I want to see what is at the bottom of this mine... Have you been down there yourself?"

"No," said the manager, "I don't like deep mines. I try to avoid going down them whenever possible, gives me the creeps."

Stone thought about that comment for a moment, "That's an odd statement from a miner,"

The manager spread his gloved hands, "Had an accident in a gold mine Earth-side a few years ago, I guess it made me wary of deep shaft mines. Mining on the moon is mostly open cut so I don't have to go down shafts. My foremen usually perform those site inspections for me."

Susan turned back to the tunnel entrance "Let's get back then. There is something I want to look at in your minerals laboratory."

As the tractor Headed back down the road, Stone looked at Susan with a puzzled expression.

"Later," she said, holding a gloved finger to her lips and nodding at the back of Simmonds head."

Arriving at Armstrong, they cycled through the airlocks and removed their suits. Back in the Mine Manager's office Susan asked if she could use the minerals lab to look at her samples

Simmons smiled, "Be my guest, but please speak to the duty technician first. They are a touchy bunch and don't like people messing with their equipment; better you ask them to process your samples for you."

"I do that, and thanks, for everything today, Mike. It has been a most interesting trip. Oh, by the way when can we be fitted for our mining suits?"

"Will tomorrow morning be Ok?"

"Fine." said Susan. Then turning to Stone, she nodded to the door and started to leave,

"Yes, thanks," said Stone. Shaking Simmonds hand, "see you tomorrow, say about 0730 local time?"

Closing the Mine Manager's door, they walked down the corridor for about 50 metres and stopped in front of a door marked 'Mineral Assay Laboratory.' They knocked and walked in. The room was typical of any analysis laboratory with two long benches on which sat several instruments, including microscopes, centrifuges, spectrophotometers, an electron microscope and the more mundane grinding and mixing equipment.

Seated at one of the instruments was a young dark-haired man in his middle twenties. Susan thought he was quite attractive, and it showed on her face. "Hello," said Susan. "The Mining Manager sent me here to ask you to look at these samples." Smiling sweetly, she took two small rock chips from her pocket and held them out to him.

The young man frowned. "You'll have to submit a written and authorised analysis request, I should be able to get to it in about a week," He held out a form to her.

Susan looked a little hurt and said, "This really is important for both me and the Company. Simonds said that I could use your spectrometers and radiometric analysers, but he suggested it would be better if you performed the analysis yourself. Of course, any advantages to the Company will be credited to you."

She broadened her smile and pouted her lips. It was too much for the young man. He softened and asked, "Where did these samples come from?"

"The new mine site, the one about thirty minutes from here."

"Ah, that will be Site – 23, also known as *Deep Cut*."

"I took these samples from the mine earlier today." said Susan,

Meanwhile Stone had been wandering around the lab looking at the various pieces of equipment. The young man swung around. "Don't touch," he said. Turning back to Susan with an interested look, he continued. "Sorry I was caught up with an urgent analysis for my boss. My name is Tom Williams… and you are?"

"Susan, Susan Stone … pleased to meet you Tom. Now about these samples … can you run a spectral analysis and if possible give me a mineral classification?"

"It will take about three hours to run, preparation time etc."

"Thank you Tom you are most helpful. Perhaps we can meet later for a drink or two."

"That will be good. If you come back in about three hours I should have the information you want."

Susan smiled and turned towards the door. Stone waved goodbye and followed his wife.

When they were outside, Stone mimicked his wife's voice. "Perhaps we can meet later, Tom."

She laughed, "Jealous?"

They headed down the corridor to the domestic area and entered the canteen. Several people were already enjoying a meal, including Springfield and Fisher. Strolling over, Stone pulled out a chair and sat, while Susan went to the servery.

Stone related the events of their tour of the mine site, ending with the trip down the deep shaft. Susan came back just as Stone had finished.

"Hi, guys," said Susan. "Honey, you go get something to eat."

She turned to Springfield, "How did you guys get on with Haslop?"

"A very interesting tale," said Springfield, similar in many ways to the other interviews, especially because when he was interviewed before he failed to mention his connection with Lim. We asked him why he did not mention the packages and also asked him what he did with them. His answer was, that he thought we already knew about the packages and so he only told us that he adjusted the manifest to balance the extra load so that the accelerator and lunar escape burn would be compensated for. Then he would load the packages into the Shuttle's cargo bay, with a false load-documentation. We also asked him what was the average weight that he had to make allowances for and he told us that on average the weight varied between five and ten kilograms, although there was an extraordinary consignment of two packages of 14 kilograms each. A considerable off-set ... and that was on the shuttle that crashed."

Fisher leaned forward and took over. "I did ask him one pertinent question, how was he able to adjust the load weight and feed the information into the launch program. He said that he transmitted the modified load parameters to a Company programmer named Mason who worked in Canada. Mason would then adjust the loads remotely and reset the computers to compensate for the additional mass. He also modified the launch sequence program to effectively hide the extra weight. Eventually Mason wrote a second program that was installed into the on-base Load Control computer, side by side with the standard Load Control program. This new program would automatically offset and hide elicit cargos and dump the added mass onto the standard program. This negated the need to send data Earth-side. I told Haslop that we already knew about Mason's involvement, and went on to explain that his family had already been secured. I also told him Mason was currently being shipped to Armstrong to get a firsthand look at the modified launch system to try and figure out what went wrong with the first Shuttle. I have to say, he is extremely worried that his modifications may have contributed to the launch failure."

"Interesting," said Susan. "How was he able to upload modified programs into the three on-board Launch computers without it being noticed?"

"We haven't figured that out yet; I assume we will find that out when we re-interview Haslop."

Stone returned with a piled plate. "Did I miss anything vital?"

Susan reached for a piece of cheese on Stone's plate, and popped it into her mouth.

"Mmm I'll tell you the full details later after lunch; but not much that we haven't guessed already. Basically, Haslop modified the cargo mass on the Load Computer using a combination of a new program provided by Mason and the standard Load program. Then the data was downloaded to the on-board Launch computers. I think we are close to solving the problem of the first shuttle crash. I am guessing, but I'll bet that an error was made in the weight calculations or in a program modification altered the voting sequence for the computers, thus causing them to miss additional mass."

Stone was suddenly alert, his mouth full of food, he gulped the food down and interrupted. "Wait a moment, what weights are we talking about here."

"Oh, anything from five to eighteen kilos." replied Susan.

Stone thoughtful, "That amount of additional mass is very unlikely to cause a catastrophic launch failure. When I last interviewed the Launch Controller he said it would take discrepancies of twenty to thirty pounds to make any appreciable difference to an acceleration rate that could cause the shuttle to fail to reach its launch velocity. Even then, it still does not answer why the fail-safe computers did not detect the low acceleration rate until too late in the launch sequence."

"Maybe we will have to wait until Mason gets here and get him to review his modification on site," Susan suggested.

Stone hurriedly finished his meal and got up. "Let's go and find out what your new boyfriend has found out about your rock samples." Susan made a face and rose from the table.

"Did I miss something?" said Springfield with a grin.

"Don't bother asking," replied Susan.

Hooking her arm round Stone's elbow, Susan led the way from the canteen. Just before getting to the laboratory they bumped into Tom, the lab technician, who was heading for the mine manager's office holding a pseudo-paper report. Stopping he looked excitedly at Susan. "I was just going to the boss's office to show him the spectral and radiometric analysis results. Where exactly did you get those samples from?"

"From the deep mine about one kilometre in."

"You know what you've got there, don't you?"

"I can guess," replied Susan. "What have you found?"

Tom laughed, "I have found the impossible — high levels of carbon in a matrix structure similar but not exactly like Kimberlite."

Stone looked puzzled, "Kimberlite, what the hell is Kimberlite?"

Tom held up the report, "A volcanic lava named after the rock structure found in the Kimberly diamond mines. It's an extruded funnel-like lava structure known as a pipe in which, in South Africa at least, diamonds can be found. The moon has extremely low levels of carbon in its crust and surface soil, so this finding is quite unique. The last suspected volcanic eruption was estimated at 25 million years ago, but usually lava flows are spread out on the surface and contain low carbon levels, rather than in a pipe formation, a volcanic vent. However the question still remains as to the carbon source?"

Stone looked at Susan, "I think I am beginning to see a developing picture."

Susan smiled, "Ten years ago as part of my general engineering degree there was a very basic geology lecture regarding bedrock structures. At the University we were shown various basalt and igneous sample and how these rock structures could affect construction techniques. One of the samples on display was Kimberlite that actually had a small diamond embedded in it. When I saw the rock surface in the mine it triggered a memory of that long-forgotten lecture. I recognised a similarity, it was a very lucky guess."

Stone took the report from Tom's hand and looked at it for a moment. "Tom, can you keep this to yourself for a couple of days? It may be very important to our investigations. The less people who know about this the better … just a couple of days, Ok?"

Tom looked torn with indecision, then Susan placed her hand on his shoulder. "Please, Tom. It really is very important to me to keep this quiet at least until tomorrow." Tom nodded, "Ok, but just for twenty four hours. This will make scientific headlines and I am keen to be the first to file a report."

"Susan nodded, I understand. This could make your name, yes?"

"Oh indeed," replied Tom.

"Thanks, Tom," said Susan. "Would you like that drink now?"

"That is an excellent idea," said Tom, beaming a smile at Susan.

Stone raised his eyes heavenward and clapped Tom on the shoulder.

"Let's go then." Tom stopped, looking disappointedly from Susan to Stone, shrugged his shoulders, smiled and followed them to the bar.

The bar was tastefully decorated in a material that looked like wood panelling. The lighting was subdued, low tables and comfortable seats scattered the area and soft background music completed the impression of an Earth-side, high end night club. The bar itself was set into one wall. Even the barman fitted the picture, dressed in a striped apron and sporting a large handlebar moustache he stood studiously polishing glasses. The obvious aim of the setting was to provide a soothing area in which to relax after a day's work.

Stone and Tom sat at one of the tables, Susan came from the bar carrying a tray with three glasses of locally made beer, courtesy of the hydroponics section. Placing the tray on the table and sitting down, then passing a glass to Tom, she said, "Tom, have you ever seen rock samples similar to the ones you tested today?"

"No that's the point. If this is what I think it is then we really need to go deeper into the mine tunnel; I'm guessing, down perhaps a further kilometre or two where pressure can do its work.

"As you know, the actual pressure required to act on carbon deposits to produce diamonds is immense. Normally diamonds are formed at extremely high temperatures and pressures. On Earth diamonds can form in the mantle layer and an eruption brings them to the surface contained in what is known as a pipe. There is also a theory that impacts by a very large solar body, such as an asteroid, could provide the temperature and pressure needed to produce diamonds.

"In this case it could be a combination of both. There is a theory that the moon was originally part of Earth and a large planet-sized body side-swiped the Earth and produced a molten planetoid that has now condensed into out moon. So in the past the moon may have had a mantle layer. We also know the moon has had volcanic activity in the very distant past. Perhaps this pipe-like material that was formed in the initial impact was forced up to the near surface. Or perhaps this was a product of a large impact by an asteroid-sized body and subsequently buried over millions of years. It's all speculation. What we do know is that we must go out to the deep mine as soon as possible, and look more closely.

CHAPTER 14

Two days later, having been fitted with miners' vacuum suits, they drove out to the deep mine site. Entering the on-site mine office Tom, Stone and Susan removed their helmets and gloves, looked around and spotted Anthony Pritchard the mine foreman. He got up from his console and held out his hand. "Welcome, the boss has told me a lot about you, including that you helped at the last crash site and did a very impressive job. Sad about Pauline though; she was well liked by all at Armstrong and we will miss her. Please come in and take off your kit and have some coffee."

Susan Smiled back and shook Pritchard's hand. Pritchard looked at Stone, "And you must be Agent Stone, yes?"

Stone looked appraisingly at Pritchard, the man was tall with a solid frame, about 45 -50 years of age, dark hair greying at the edges.

Susan cut in before Stone could answer, "Thanks for the offer, but we are a bit pressed for time. I would really like to review the site where Eric Carlsen disappeared. It would be very helpful if you could arrange for us to go there as soon as possible." The foreman nodded affably. "Ok that suits me."

"You know Tom?" said Stone.

"Yes of course, how are you Tom?" "Good thanks, Mr. Pritchard."

Prichard pointed to the couch. "Please take a seat and have a coffee while I suit up." He turned away and headed for the back of the office and grabbing a vacuum suit from the rack, entered the change area.

Tom walked over to the small kitchen area and prepared three cups of coffee. As they were finishing their coffee Susan looked across at the change area and said to Stone, "He seems helpful," and was about to say something else when the foreman reappeared.

Ten minutes later when Pritchard had finished his final suit check they replaced their helmets and gloves. Then they walked into the airlock. Prichard closed the inner door and cycled the outer hatch. They stepped out onto the lunar surface. Looking out over the stark landscape, they could see the sun rising over a nearby mountain. The suits' air-conditioners' kicked in as the temperature started to rise. Pritchard waved his hand towards the deep mine opening. "Sunrise, we should hurry" he said, then added, "The suits can handle the heat but the aircon units tend to be a little power hungry, which can reduce our work-time."

After entering the mine they walked down the tunnel for about thirty minutes. Susan started to look more closely at the walls, seeing the same ore formation that had she collected on the earlier trip. She pointed out one formation to Tom, who took a sample.

At the one and a half kilometre marker the downward gradient of the tunnel sharply increased and Susan's suit temperature gauge dropped several degrees. They continued on for about another two kilometres. Pritchard was lagging behind them by about one hundred metres. Stone put his hand up and waved Pritchard forward. "What's the matter with the man, he is supposed to be leading us!"

Just then two mine workers appeared round the curve of the tunnel. Stone turned to Susan, "I don't like this." As he spoke, the two men came at them with remarkable speed for men wearing suits. They carried what looked like rock chisels. Susan froze for a brief second, then exploded into a blur of movement. The first man headed towards Stone, his face could be clearly seen through the visor was contorted with effort but never made it past Susan. Flinging out her arm at face height she brought the metal part of her glove into sharp contact with his faceplate. Her speed and power was such that the man's helmet visor cracked, then the glass exploded outward. The man convulsed and dropped to his knees, toppling forward and gasping like a fish out of water, his body jerking in agony as he desperately tried to draw air into his lungs.

The second man was on the downward stroke with his chisel aimed at Susan's chest. She sprang backward and the man staggered forward into Stone who grabbed the arm with the chisel and pivoted, redirecting the blow so that the chisel tore into the man's suit at waist height. The effect of suit decompression on both men was clearly visible. Their faces puffed out and blood spots appeared on the skin, their eyes bulging as they fought for breath.

"That was messy" said Stone; but he was talking to a blur as Susan's Earth-trained muscles powered her towards the fleeing foreman. Tom was frozen with a look of horror on his face, gazing after Susan.

Pritchard had no chance. Hampered by the weight of his suit and his weak muscles after working in low gravity for two years he could only manage a brief trot before Susan cannoned into his back, pinning him to the ground. Stone came up behind her as she was about to tear off the man's helmet. "Stop, Susan, Stop! … We need him!"

Susan released her grip on Pritchard's helmet and stood up, looking down at the clearly terrified man. He had just witnessed the death of two of his strongest workers. Through his helmet visor they could see his face twitching with fear. Stone knelt down beside him. "Listen very carefully to what I'm about to say. You have already seen what my partner is capable of, and I can assure you I will release her to kill you in the most painful way possible; slow decompression should do it. Nod if you understand!" Pritchard nodded inside his helmet. "Now take us to the place where my colleague disappeared. And also I believe you have a package for me." Prichard quavered, "I can take you to where we lost the maintenance man, but I know nothing about a package."

"Ok, Honey, kill him! He is no use to us now," said Stone in a quiet voice." The foreman tried to struggle to his feet, but Susan had him tight and started to reach for his helmet interlock.

"Ok, Ok!" said Pritchard, "I'll do it!" He stood staggering a little then headed down the tunnel. As he passed his two ex-employees he looked down at them and shuddered.

By this time, Tom had decided that he would return to the mine-site office. "I feel sick. Sorry, I need to go back." Susan patted his shoulder, Tom flinched away, turned and half ran toward the mine entrance.

They travelled on for what appeared to be an hour heading deeper into the mine. At about four kilometres in Pritchard stopped and pointed to a piece of machinery. "That was where he was last seen by our mining crew."

"I don't suppose that it was the same two that we have just retired?"

"As a matter of fact, yes, but I know nothing about what happened to him."

Stone looked through his suit visor at the man's eyes, then turned, "Susan?" I think he's lying."

Pritchard replied, "I'm not, I swear to you. I knew about the packages and I guessed about what happened to the maintenance guy, but I swear I had nothing to do with his disappearance."

Stone thought for a moment, "Let's say I believe you … How come these same two guys just tried to kill me and my partner."

"I swear I didn't know they would be here, but when I saw them attack you I panicked."

"Ok, what about the package? … Give now, or stay down her with your men." Even through the faceplate of the suit, it was clear that the man had given up. He shrugged and went to a locker set in the side of the rock face. Tapping a combination on the keyboard, he opened the locker and extracted two bags. "Here, I'm a dead man now, anyway."

Stone took the bags which were so tightly sealed that he could not open them with gloved hands. "Let's go." Said Stone, as he hoisted the heavy bags onto his shoulder. With Pritchard leading followed by Susan, with Stone bringing up the rear, they headed back up the tunnel. Suddenly Susan stopped. "Wait," she said. "Look at this rock formation here." She took out her small chisel and hammer and attacked the wall, without warning, a large piece of rock fell away from the surface, revealing a large rough object half buried in the wall. She eased it out; it was what looked like an opaque dirty piece of glass about one centimetre across its surface and two centimetres thick. "This!" she said triumphantly, holding up the dirty rock, "is what it's all about. This crappy piece of carbon is worth, on the industrial market alone, about one hundred thousand credits. Not bling quality, but good enough for industrial use." She smiled to herself, "Let's go."

They headed back up to the surface, just in time to watch the sun drop below a mountain and the lights come on around the site. On entering the mine-site office, Susan pushed the foreman onto the seat. She stopped dead in her tracks. "Where's Tom?" Stone went into the change area and the small sleeping room. Tom was not there.

"He should be back by now. Where is he?" Stone cycled the airlock and went out, and began to search. Several miners were busy loading a huge ore truck. They took no notice as Stone came up behind them.

Stone tapped the nearest miner on the helmet to attract his attention, then using his communicator he said, "A young man came up out of the deep mine some time ago, have you seen him?" The miner pointed over to the shower block, "He went in there I think, hasn't come out yet." "Thanks'."

With that, Stone moved quickly to the building. Worried about Tom, he did not think to look behind him, which was a mistake. As he reached for the hatch control, he felt a hard blow to his helmet. He staggered forward and someone pinned his arms to his side. He twisted and managed to get face to face with his assailant. Reaching round behind the man he got his hands on the air conditioning unit. He pulled down hard to bring his attacker off balance. Although the man was tall and heavy built, he had been working at Armstrong for many years and his strength could not match Earth-trained muscles. He toppled backwards, and like a turtle on its back, was helpless.

Just then, the airlock to the shower block opened, and another man appeared and jumped high landing on Stone's shoulder pack. Stone attempted the same manoeuvre that had worked on the first man, but this new assailant was obviously fresh from Earth. He swung an iron bar at Stone's faceplate Stone turned his body just in time to take the blow on the side of his helmet. However it knocked him off balance and he landed on his back. Looking up, he saw his death as the metal bar swung down towards his face. He closed his eyes expecting death. Nothing happened. He opened his eyes again and the figure had gone. Standing in the same place was Susan. She reached down and helped him up. "Husband, I can't leave you for a minute." He smiled, then looked down at the bloody mess that had been his assailant. The other man was still stranded on his back.

They cycled the hatch and entered the Shower block. In one corner sat Tom, his helmet on the floor beside him. His mouth was wide open as if screaming, a terrified expression contorting his face. A knife handle protruded from under his chin; the rest of the blade had gone up through his throat and into his brain.

Susan felt herself shake with remorse; if only she had not involved him. She reached for the knife and tenderly removed it, stroking the side of Tom's face. She stood up and cycled the airlock, dropping onto the lunar surface. By the time Stone had caught up with her, Susan was standing over the man on the ground. Through the glass of her helmet her face appeared ugly and twisted as she felt a huge rage build up within her. Without warning, "Bastard!" she screamed, "Bastard!" as she slammed the long blade deep into the man's torso, over and over again until she was exhausted. Gradually her rage subsided, leaving her panting and gasping for breath. Stone had come up behind her, crooning softly. With infinite care, he slowly took the knife away from his wife's gloved hand, and dropped it onto the lunar surface. The suited figure on the ground convulsed once, arching its back while the inside of the faceplate suddenly turned red as blood filled the helmet from the punctured torso.

Stone gently led Susan back to the office. Pritchard was tied by cable straps to his chair. He looked up as they entered, fear showing in his eyes. After taking off her helmet, Stone cupped Susan's face in both his hands.

She slowly recovered, her breath heaving in great gasps while the tears rolled down her face. "Poor boy, he had some much to live for." She reached up and stroked Stone's face. "But that's not what scares me." The reason I cry is because that could have been you, and I was not there to save you!" She shouted the last words. Stone said nothing; he just continued to hold her face until the heaving sorrow had abated.

CHAPTER 15

The return journey to Armstrong was uneventful. Susan drove, as she was qualified on most vacuum plant equipment. They had already called Fisher and explained what had happened. Fisher was waiting at the vehicle bay airlock when they arrived. "Hi Harry, Susan .... What a mess, bodies piling up everywhere.

"No time now, Karl, we need to get this bird locked up, and open these," Stone held up the bags.

"What's in there," said Fisher.

"Not sure yet, but whatever is in these bags may be responsible for a good deal of our troubles."

Stone and Susan had just settled themselves in the Security office when Fisher and his sergeant returned. Settling himself into his chair, and pouring four glasses of good bourbon, he rolled the whiskey round the inside of his glass.

Ok, Harry, what have we got now?" he said, pointing at the two bags sitting untouched on his desk.

Stone got up and retrieved one of the bags. Using his pocket knife he sliced into the side of the bag. He tipped the bag over the desk and a shower of sparkling stones poured out.

"Bloody hell!" said Fisher. Even Susan was astonished. These weren't crude industrial grade stones unlike the one she had found. These were high grade bling, not one stone under one and a half carats.

Stone picked up a large gem and looking closely at it murmured, "One thing is for sure; weight for weight, this is the best way to move large amounts of money by spacecraft. Now we know the reason behind the cover-up, all we need know is who are the main buyers and suppliers. But why the reactor sabotage?"

As he was speaking, Miles and Springfield entered. "I think I can answer that," said Miles. It will cost you two of your excellent Bourbons. Fisher got up and poured two more glasses.

Miles seated himself on the long couch, took a sip and smiled. "It is all to do with a simple Senate election for the presidential seat. I have long suspected that some of our masters were somehow involved in all of this. The LPS was too simple to be believable. Nothing about the organisation made sense as well as that, Stevens in Ottawa has come up with some interesting news; the presidential election is almost hung with both China and the European Union holding the casting votes. But that is not the most interesting point. The principal candidates include the CEO of ... yes, you've guessed it ... the CEO of Transglobal. The other candidate is even more interesting — our own chief officer and senior public servant, the Inspector General of the Criminal Investigation Service."

Stone listened with a sudden dawning the intuitive leap he had been waiting for. "Which one of them is bribing the Senate and who in the Senate is receiving the bribe?"

"A very astute observation, grasshopper. Now you're thinking. But it is not one person that needs to be bribed. The whole Senate of a given country must vote unanimously." Miles rubbed his hands together, "I think it's time we paid a visit to our two guests from Earth, what do you think?"

Stone drained his glass, stood up and pointed at Miles, "You knew all along, didn't you?" Miles smiled, "I had some inkling of what was going on, I just didn't know where the funding was coming from. I needed to set up a misdirection so that I could investigate the matter with a credible reason to involve CIS. Investigating the LPS was an obvious choice. As luck would have it although they are a crank organisation, someone there used the veiled threat to end mining by doing a bit of mild sabotage to the reactor. This prompted the Senate Security Council to order us to investigate. So after the reactor incident I sent in our first agent, then I sent you in with the Guess questions, you see, I needed a set of circumstances that would bring the villains out into view. You achieved that Stone, and I am eternally grateful to you and sorry that I had to mislead you."

"Transporting diamonds is a cheap way to move money but it does not make sense to destroy your means of transport, so where does the shuttle disasters fit into the matrix?" asked Fisher.

Miles stood up and drained his glass. "That is one of the last questions we need to answer. I agree that to destroy your only means of shipping is illogical, but I'm sure another intuitive leap will fill in the blanks. A clue though, I don't think the first accident was deliberate sabotage, more of a cock-up. Over to you grasshopper."

Stone stood and opened the door, beckoning to Susan, "You watch too many movies, Miles. But I hear you, a little more digging is needed."

After leaving the office they headed for the launch bay. "I have an idea that may solve our first shuttle disaster. We need to talk with the launch controller, the one that programs the weight factors."

A few minutes later they entered the control room, where the launch controller, Maurice Haslop was seated at his console. Stone and Susan walked across the room and sat on either side of him.

"Mr. Maurice Haslop?" asked Stone.

The man looked nervous. "Yes that's me, what can I do for you?"

"Let me introduce myself, my name is Harry Stone and this is my wife Susan, we both work for the CIS."

Haslop looked worried, "I have already been interviewed by CIS yesterday a Mr Gibson."

"That would be my boss." said Stone. "I understand that you have been told that you family is safe and has been placed under our protection. Am I right?"

"Yes, Mr Gibson told me that yesterday. Has something happened?" he asked nervously, his eyes flicking from one to the other.

Stone smiled, "No, nothing new has happened. Relax, they are still safe."

Haslop smiled with relief.

Stone continued, "May I call you Maurice?" Haslop nodded. Stone leaned forward and placed a finger on the screen panel. "Maurice, can show me how you program the manifest loads into the on-board launch control computer from this console?"

Haslop smiled again, "Sure, I'll do anything I can to help, as I told Mr Gibson."

Stone leaned back in his chair. "Good, thank you. Now during your last interview with Mr Gibson, you admitted to hiding the mass of an extra and illegal cargo, in a way that allowed the Shuttle's launch computer to calculate the correct launch weight. Can you show me how that was that done?"

"Sure," replied Maurice, much relieved. He tapped the keyboard, and a standard data entry screen appeared. "Before we can add in the hidden load, we first have to enter the standard known mass of the Shuttle itself. The standard weight for the Lunar Shuttle is 63,502.932 kilograms, the mass of passengers and crew is 600 kg. We now add the mass of the primary cargo, say 1100 Kg." He stopped, "To save time, why don't, I call up the last load data, Ok?"

Stone nodded, "Sounds good."

"This is the data from the last Shuttle, the one that killed Captain Hicks. It was never launched."

He tapped the keyboard and a completed data entry screen

Lunar Shuttle Load Launch Mass Data Entry	
Shuttle Registered Number: LS A412798 Launch Date: 2109/05/03 EST 21:17 Pilot Captain Hicks	
Item	Mass In Kilograms
Shuttle Launch weight	63,502.93
Fuel	600.50
Crew 1	62.35
Pax 0	0

Primary Cargo He-3	900.58
Commercial Cargo 1 Interplanetary Fuel Federal	1000.34
Commercial Cargo 2	
Total Mass	66,066.7

Press Enter to upload to Shuttle on-board Launch Computer

"Thanks, Maurice, now, during your last interview, you admitted to hiding the mass of the illicit cargo, but in such a way as to allow the launch computer to arrive at the correct mass. How was that achieved?"

The controller looked a little embarrassed. "It has to do with the new program provided by Arnold Mason, watch this …" He started the process again. "Before we enter all the data, the screen looks exactly the same, yes?" Stone nodded.

"The data is first downloaded into the on-board Launch computer *before* we add the hidden cargo." Stone nodded again. Maurice tapped a couple of keys and brought up the modified program, "Now watch as I enter the hidden cargo into the modified program. Now let's add 100 kilograms for the hidden cargo." He entered 100 into the entry screen of the modified program and pressed the return key. The manifest list once again appeared.

Lunar Shuttle Load Launch Mass Data Entry Shuttle Registered Number: LS A412798 Launch Date: 2109/05/03 EST 21:17 Pilot Captain Hicks	
Item	Mass In Kilograms
Shuttle Launch weight	63,502.93
Fuel	600.50
Crew 1	72.35

Pax 0	0
Primary Cargo He-3	930.58
Commercial Cargo 1 Interplanetary Fuel Federal	1060.34
Commercial Cargo 2	
Total Mass	66,166.7

Press Enter to upload to Shuttle on-board Launch Computer

"You will note that the program has distributed the extra mass over the whole manifest, with the exception of the Shuttle mass and fuel load, but the extra hidden cargo itself does not appear. This extra mass is only presented to the Shuttle's on-board launch computer. It does not appear on the Flight Control computer. Remember, we download the genuine figures to the Shuttle before we add the extra load. What you are seeing is what the Shuttle's computer sees, not what is recorded here at flight control." He smiled and sat back, "Clever, yes?"

Stone looked at the screen again and said, "Very ingenious ... One last question, what would happen if the load was 100 kilograms overweight and you had altered the monitoring process of the launch computers?"

Haslop thought for a moment, "That much weight overload would probably exceed the launch capability, and if the computer voting system had been interfered with, the low acceleration rate might not be detected until too late. Because the computers believed that they were dealing with a certain mass with a certain calculated momentum, they might try braking, In the case of 100kg overweight the momentum from this extra mass might not allow for safe braking before the end of the rail, so the computers might try to accelerate to launch speed and fire the emergency thruster. It would be a close thing. I believe that the crashed Shuttle in question was short of its launch-escape velocity when it reached the end of the rail. I think it may have left the rail nose down as the emergency thruster fired, but we have not been to locate any remains of the computer system, or the pilot for that matter.

I guess we will have to wait for the official report from the crash investigation team; they say it may be one or two years before they have any conclusive answer." He paused again to think. "The telemetry from the crashed Shuttle was recorded in the flight control centre, and does show that the craft was considerably short of its launch speed when the on-board launch computers voted to decelerate and abort. Then about one second later, the abort was cancelled and acceleration resumed. Unfortunately not enough speed was recovered for a successful launch." He stood up, "Perhaps if we give this new information to the accident team it would speed the investigation."

Stone held up his hand, "No, that would not be wise at this time. We are after all only speculating. Besides, I don't want you to speak to anybody about what we've discussed today."

The Controller nodded in agreement. "That suits me."

After leaving the control room, Stone took Susan's arm and led her to the canteen.

Susan went to the counter and collected two coffees. As they sat waiting, Stone leaned forward and whispered, "Susan, I have turned on the anti-bug device, but keep your voice down."

She nodded. "You are on to something?"

"I sure am. Miles was right, I now believe that there was no intent to sabotage the first shuttle. I'm firmly convinced that the cause of the crash was a combination of stupidity and bad luck. The first thing that twigged me was the information the controller gave when first interviewed you remember he said that it would require about a twenty to thirty pounds overload to appreciably affect a launch?" Susan sipped her coffee, "Yes."

Stone smiled, "Well, that's strange because, load weights are in kilograms, getting the picture?"

Susan nodded, "I think I know where you are going with this … go on."

Stone resumed, "What would cause a computer program to calculate a lower mass load?"

Susan thought for a moment, "Incorrect data input?"

"You would think so, but we watched Haslop enter that data correctly, so what went wrong?"

Susan shook her head, "You remember the Canadian programmer what's his name?"

Stone replied, Arnold Mason, he was due in on the next shuttle to review the program, but I don't think we need him now. Better he stays where he is, rather than risk another person." Stone rubbed his forehead, "I think I understand most of what went wrong, but I need to think about it a little more."

Suddenly, he stood up knocking his chair over, "Got it! I need to go back to the Flight Control office again right now." He rushed out of the canteen. Susan shook her head, finished her coffee and followed Stone to the flight control section.

When she arrived Stone was already bent over the console. She leaned over beside him, and what she saw made a lot of sense. After all, she was an aerospace engineer. It was the crashed Shuttle's operational and maintenance manual. She also noted that all weights and measures were in American standard pounds, feet and inches, etc. That surprised her because the American aerospace industry had joined the rest of the world in using metric measures some twenty years ago. However this shuttle was twenty two years old.

Then she understood. This was the oldest ship in the fleet, and its initial design specifications were in US standard units being a modification of the old imperial measurements. She read further on about the load parameters and they were still in pounds; even the power source was measured in pounds of thrust. However, the ground flight control computer understood this and made all the necessary conversions from kilos to pounds automatically, before feeding the data to the on-board computer of this particular Shuttle.

Stone turned to Haslop, "Maurice, I want you to imagine you are entering data for the crashed Shuttle. How would you do it?"

"The process is slightly different for this Shuttle, as all loads are measured in pounds. The original program will recognise this Shuttle's registration code and will automatically convert all mass entered from kilograms to pounds. I would still enter all the data as before in kilograms. I would add the standard mass set for the shuttle including fuel. Again, let's assume that the shuttle is full and the mass of passengers is 600 kg. We now add the mass of the primary cargo, say 1100 kg.

Primary Cargo Mass	1100	2452.0849
Passenger mass	600	1322.7736
Total		3774.8585

Next we download to the on-board computer. "Then we switch to the modified program and add the 50 kg of hidden cargo. Haslop entered the 50 Kilos and pressed the return key.

Primary Cargo Mass	1130 kg	2482.0849 Lb
Passenger mass	620 kg	1342.7736 Lb
Total		3824.8585 Lb

Stone pointed to the screen, "Do you see anything strange?"

Maurice peered at the screen, "Oh my god, what's happened? That's wrong, the total is incorrect! There is about a 50 pounds or about 22 kilograms, missing"

When Stone examined the code for the modified program he soon discovered that no such conversion had taken place. The Canadian programmer, knowing that the load unit for Lunar Shuttles was expressed in kilograms, assumed that all input figures fed into this program would be in kilos. That meant, that if the figure 50 was entered, then his program would assume that that it was indeed 50 kilograms and pass the figure to the Shuttle's launch computer. The input figure 50 was in effect 50 kilograms, but when the modified program passed the data to the main on-line flight computer it appeared as 50 pounds. This would then this would be evenly split between the other items on the manifest which was still displayed, on the Ground computer at least, as kilograms.

Stone pocketed his computer, "I think I understand now. We have a simple calculation error. Maurice, is that a sufficient difference to abort a launch?"

The controller nodded, "Yes, but it should not have been fatal; the acceleration deficit should have been picked up by the computers during the first couple of kilometres of launch The accident could have been avoided as the mass deficit should have only made a moderate difference," He considered for a moment, "Also, why was this error not detected by the investigator who asked demonstrate the system yesterday?"

"Which investigator was that?" said Susan.

"The one that said he was taking over from you"

Stone nodded, "That would be Dixon. One last question: What can cause a malfunction in the voting sequence of the computers?"

"That's nearly impossible, but there is one situation that can cause a problem. It requires exceeding the load capability of the shuttle by a considerable amount and a manual over-ride. For instance, if someone wanted for some reason to override the launch procedure, he or she would have to reprogram the monitoring system to ignore acceleration deficit leading up to the actual launch sequence. But even then, the computers should have aborted the launch sooner."

"The poor bastard," Stone said, thinking not of Haslop but of the pilot who as per usual had assumed that all units of measurement were already converted by the ground load controller's computer. However no such conversion had taken place for the added load and the Shuttle was overweight by at least 23 kilograms.

Had he been piloting a more modern Shuttle, that used metric unit of measurement, there would have been no problem. The load on his Shuttle had previously been converted from kilograms to pounds so the figures would match. However the modified program produced no such conversion and, as far as the hidden load was concerned, the inputs were all seen by the pilot and on-board computer as pounds.

Stone sat on the edge of the desk, "So we now know that the payload was defective. But who modified the launch computer redundancy system."

Susan closed her eyes, "Who has access to the Shuttle's on-board system before the launch, besides the load and launch controllers and possibly the engineering section?"

Stone stood, "Just about anyone involved in the launch process who has to input data to the system. Possibly even down to the flight technicians." He stopped turned to Haslop, "Can you get me a list of the personnel who worked on the Shuttle prior to launch?"

Haslop turned to his console, "Sure." After a couple of seconds, a list appeared on the screen.

Stone examined the list complete with ID photos and pointed to one photo on the screen. "I know this man. What's his trade?" Oh that's Albert Copeland, he does the final check on payloads and assists passengers when necessary. He's been with us for years, nice guy."

"Can you get him here?"

"Let me check. He comes on shift in 30 minutes. Do you want to see him now?"

Stone held up his hand, "Yes, but not here. Where's his workstation?"

"Over near the passenger terminal."

"Then we'll pay him an unannounced visit. Maurice, would contact Fisher at security and tell him that we want him outside Copeland's work station, in say forty minutes."

Haslopsat back in his chair with tears running down his face. "Did I cause the crash?" he sobbed.

Stone place a hand on his shoulder, "I don't think you can be held solely responsible. There are others more culpable than you involved." Stone straightened, "Besides, what choice did you have?" Stone looked at the shattered man, "Maurice, you have been most helpful. If it's any consolation I don't blame you for putting your family first, and I will certainly put a case for mitigating circumstances, on your behalf."

Susan, her face reflecting some concern said. "Who is this guy Copeland?"

"Someone I may have overlooked." Replied Stone. He turned to the load controller, "Thanks, Maurice."

Then took Susan's arm and they walked towards the control room door …

"Ok Stone, what else don't I know about?"

"Be patient Honey all will become clear"

Thirty five minutes later Albert Copeland entered the passenger terminal. The next Shuttle was not due to arrive for twenty hours so there were people about. He was walking quickly to his workstation, he looked at his watch — he was late. At first he did not notice the tall powerfully built man walking towards him. When the man got closer he recognised him and smiled. The man smiled back and put his arm around Copeland's shoulder and spoke quietly into his ear. Copeland looked frantically around, but nobody seemed to notice the small drama taking place.

Holding him firmly, the big man guided his smaller companion to a maintenance access air lock. Copland wriggled in the big man's grasp, but he was too strong. Arriving at the airlock, the man tapped a code onto the control pad. The hatch swung open. The man shifted his grip on Copeland's head dragging him into the airlock space then placing his hand round the small man's throat and using thumb and forefinger he applied pressure to the carotid arteries.

Copeland began to panic and twisted furiously from side to side. The big man continued to hold his grip and gradually the struggling slowed and stopped as Copeland's legs buckled under him. He sagged to the ground. The big man turned his back and walked out of the airlock, casually pressing another contact that closed the inner hatch.

Copeland by this time had recovered somewhat, he lifted himself off the floor and reached for the inner control panel and pressed the inner hatch contact. Nothing happened. He tried again to open the hatch by frantically pressing and repressing the hatch interlock. Again nothing happened, the inner door remained closed. He raced to the door in panic and pressed his face against the viewport, his mouth working but no sound came through the thick door.

The big man shrugged his shoulders, smiled, and touched a contact that started to cycle the outer hatch leading onto the lunar surface. Air hissed out of the airlock space slowly exposing Copeland to near-vacuum. He looked pleadingly through the window, his face pressed against the glass, a trickle of blood in the corner of his bulging eyes, his lungs working furiously to feed oxygen to his already failing body. The outer door swung open. Copeland's face puffed and contorted, his eyes wide with terror, still pressed against the glass. Blood oozed out of the corner of one eye and from his nose. His body started to spasm with the effort to breathe, his tongue tingled as the saliva in his mouth started to boil off into vacuum. He opened his mouth wide as he tried to scream, but no sound issued. Slowly his face, distorted in an agony of regret for his lost family, slid down the glass, leaving a long track of fresh blood that evaporated almost immediately.

The big man sighed, smiled, and simply walked away from the airlock, unnoticed by the few people around him. Ten minutes later, the emergency alarm sounded, and Stone and Susan, waiting at Copeland's workstation, knew that something was wrong.

CHAPTER 16

Stone raced out of the office followed by Susan. They immediately collided with the Security Chief, Fisher who was just entering the workstation.

"What's going on, Harry?"

Ignoring the question, Stone rushed towards the Flight Engineer's section. Susan and Fisher caught up as Max the engineer ran into Stone.

"What's the problem, Max?" enquired Stone.

"We've had a maintenance hatch malfunction, and by the look of things it could be quite bloody. We are trying to recycle the hatch now, but the interlocking system appears to be inoperative. We're sending a work team out through the Engineer's exit to assess the situation. The alarm automatically sounds when the outer door is open and someone tries to open the inner hatch. All I know is, the outer door refuses to close and the interlocking mechanism prevents the inner door from opening."

A worried expression crossed Stone's face, "You said it looked quite bloody - what do you mean?"

"The hatch door has a lot of blood splattered on the viewing port. I will have more information when the boys get a look at the hatch from the outside, but I'm guessing that someone was inside the hatch chamber when it opened to vacuum. I hope it's not one of my people."

Stone turner to Fisher, "There is nothing we can do here, let's get back to the Load Section and speak to Copeland."

Copeland was not at his workstation when the three returned.

"Late for work I guess," said Fisher. The three settled down to wait. Stone fidgeting with his computer and going over his notes. Susan reading, and Fisher pacing about.

After thirty minutes, Stone stood up and stretched, "It appears that he's not coming to work. I guess we can interview him later." Turning to Fisher he asked, "Karl, do you have his personal phone access key?"

Fisher tapped his phone wristband and brought up a list of numbers, "Yes. got it."

"Call him and tell him to come to your office." As Stone was speaking, the door opened and Max came in.

"If that's Copeland you talking about, that won't be necessary. We've just found him."

Fisher took Max's arm, "You're sure it's him?" "Difficult to be absolutely sure without DNA analysis, but the body has Copeland's identity card and some personal effects."

"Ok, Max, let's go," said Fisher. They both left leaving Susan and Stone in stunned silence.

"This is getting to be very difficult, we're running out of witnesses," said Stone.

Susan looked thoughtful. "Maybe he left something that could be useful to us in there," she said, pointing to office console and desk.

"Ok, you start going through the files while I call Miles."

Stone, tapped his wristband and spoke a number. Through the bone conducting implant behind his ear he could hear Miles' phone chiming. There was a slight pause then Miles' voice came through. "Harry? Where are you now? And what was the alarm about?"

Stone sighed "Sorry, Paul, both Susan and I usually turn off our phones when interviewing, I guess I forgot to reactivate it."

An audible hiss of exasperation echoed in Stones ear. "Never mind, we've dug up some further information that should help with a satisfactory outcome for this investigation."

Stone listened with some impatience and suddenly cut across Miles' speech, "Paul, listen! I think I know what happened to the first Shuttle. Unfortunately the man who would have been able to confirm my analysis has just been killed. That was what the alarm was all about. I believe someone shoved him out of an airlock without a suit."

The phone went silent for a moment, then, "Where are you now?"

"In the Passenger Departure area," replied Stone.

"Good, stay there. Springfield and I will be along directly. I think we can just about wrap this business up and get out of this sardine tin." The earpiece went dead.

"I got half of that," said Susan, "What does he want us to do?"

"Stay here and wait for him and Springfield. He says he has new information that may wrap up the enquiry."

"I hope so, this is becoming an increasing hazardous venture."

Just then Fisher entered. "It's him all right, no doubt. Medical ran a rapid DNA screen and it matched his stored tissue sample with a confidence of 99%."

The mention of this little device reminded Stone of the last legal wrangle that he had been involved in. When, before he met Susan, his former girlfriend had declared he was about to become a father. Stone, suspicious that he may have not been the only man in her life subjected himself to a DNA analysis. Despite repeated negative tests by the medical profession indicating someone else was the father, it had cost him nearly a year's pay in medical and legal costs to obtain a Court issued certificate declaring that he was indeed not the natural father. Ten years after this event, and thanks to this little device, it is rare for paternity cases to be heard in courts, much to the chagrin of the legal profession.

Rapid DNA analysis was now performed using a small hand held device that directly compared nucleotide sequences with a reference sample, and produced 'a match, no match' result in minutes. Not only are most police forces equipped with them but they are in great demand by the general public, particularly in cases where paternity is in question. Despite many attempts by the legal and medical professions to limit its sale to the general public, this little device is still freely available over the pharmacy counter.

Finding in favour for the sale of little DNA analyser to the general public, a World Senate High Court Judge, summed up by citing the free availability of pregnancy rapid test kits. He opined that if it is the right of all women to know if they are pregnant without medical consultation, then it is also the right of both parents to determine who the father is. The Judge also opined that since its introduction, the burden on the courts regarding paternity issues has been reduced by two thirds, saving money for both government and individuals.

Snapping out of his reverie, Stone turned to Fisher. "Ok, so we have lost yet another witness, I'm starting to think of myself as the Grim Reaper, so many people that I have come into contact with has ended up dead or injured."

Fisher patted his shoulder, "Don't be too hard on yourself, this thing seems to have a life of its own. Oh, by the way, Miles asked me to arrange a meeting with our two 'masters' in the Manager's office. They have agreed to meet you and Susan at 2000 hours, local time."

Just then, Miles and Springfield entered the room.

Miles immediately began talking. "It's time that we pooled our information. I'll go first. Springfield and I interviewed your Site Foreman at length. He finally admitted that he was being paid to organise the mining and packaging of the diamonds, he was also required to liaise with Lim Lee to deliver the packages to Albert Copeland, whose job it was to get the packages onto the Shuttle." Miles rubbed his eyes. "Unfortunately we have lost our star witness and that could cause problems in identifying the ringleaders."

"Maybe not." said Stone, "Susan and I have also been busy. It turns out that the program designed to hide unofficial payloads was defective and when applied to the older Shuttle it proved fatal. This particular spacecraft was unique. It was the first of its kind, and the last to be manufactured using the now obsolete American standard units of weight, dimensions and power. As a result, all loads travelling on this craft needed to be converted from kilograms to pounds before the data was fed into this particular Shuttle's Launch Computer."

Stone wiped his brow and continued. "In normal circumstances that conversion was performed automatically by the ground based Load Computer, then downloaded into the Shuttle's system. In this case, the unofficial program that was designed to hide cargoes assumed that all inputs to the Shuttle's Flight Computer would be in kilograms and did not apply the conversion factor. When the bogus program added the hidden weight (in kilograms) and transmitted it, the Shuttle's on-board computer assumed the weight to be in pounds."

He paused, "Actually, this is not the first time that this has happened. There was a case in last century of an old jet that ran out of fuel because of similar confusion with a metric to US standard conversion. This caused the fuelling station at the air terminal to load only half the fuel that was needed for the flight. Fortunately, in that case nobody died, thanks to some excellent piloting."

Miles asked, "Why didn't the redundant safety computers detect the unexpectedly low acceleration curve?"

"Unfortunately, the answer to that probably died with Copeland; but I suspect there was an additional cargo that weighed about 80 kilograms. Copeland almost certainly placed the extra cargo on the Shuttle and adjusted the load using the modified program for additional mass. By now the extra weight was closer to 65 or even 70 kilograms."

Springfield's eyes lit up, "That extra cargo, wouldn't be what I think it was, would it?"

"Precisely that." Said Stone, "Our missing agent!"

Miles cut in "But that would mean that the body would be have been discovered when the Shuttle arrived at Gamma 5."

"That's no problem for these people. Remember, blame would probably fall on the non-existent LPS. I'm pretty sure that the method by which our man died was by exposure to vacuum. His death may even have been set up as a Shuttle decompression accident."

Miles cut in again, "Harry, what is your theory on the modification to the launch computers?"

"I'm guessing that maybe two of the computers might have had their programs altered to accept the initial slow acceleration curve, possibly to cover the additional excess cargo mass. However, nobody imagined an almost 70 kilo overload. Again I'm guessing, but I think that someone modified Launch program in the on-board computer monitoring systems. I think that we will eventually learn that they were set to kick in as the calculated escape velocity was reached. But the extra weight slowed the craft fractionally, so that when the systems kicked in the computers working on the basis of the programmed load mass decided to terminate the launch. But there was too much momentum with the added weight, so the computers opted for an increased acceleration plus emergency boost. But as luck would have it, the deceleration caused by the initial abort attempt, made it impossible to achieve launch speed before the end of the rail was reached. The rest is history...." Stone shrugged, "Criminal activity plus bad luck. Interestingly, if the pilot had been in manual launch mode, he might have detected the sluggish acceleration, and either powered up or aborted the lunch."

"Thank you Harry, a most comprehensive explanation ... Springfield, have you organised our meeting for tonight?" asked Miles. "Done, Paul, but they're not happy."

"I take it you did not mention that I would be at the meeting?"

"No, as instructed, I told them that Stone, Susan, my sergeant and I would be present and that we wished to present a final report on the Shuttle accident."

"Good, I wish to make a surprise entrance. I think their reaction should be interesting."

Stone rose stiffly to his feet and gestured toward his wife, "Time for something to eat, Honey. It's been a long day and I'm starving, how about you, Charles?"

Springfield jumped out of his chair, "I'm with you. I've been trying to tell Miles all day that I need food."

Miles smiled, "All right, children, off you go. But don't forget to be at the Manager's office on time."

Fisher stood, "I think I'll take a walk around the Base. I'm getting to be a little jumpy these days."

As they left the room, Stone passed a note to Susan and said softly, "Honey, get this note to Max the Engineer, then join us at the canteen." Susan made to object, but Stone whispered in her ear, she smiled and nodded.

Springfield and Stone had just settled down to their meal when Susan arrived,

"Everything good?" enquired Stone,

"All good, and Max said that he will organise everything so you're not to worry. I'll skip the meal if you don't mind, low gravity and big meals are doing my figure no end of damage.

"I hadn't noticed," Stone smirked. "See you at the Manager's office in two hours, love you...." She blew him a kiss and left.

Springfield smirked, "Lucky you, wife, lover and bodyguard all in one, but I'll bet she hates housework." Stone smiled back, "Right on all counts."

CHAPTER 17

S pringfield and Stone arrived at the Manager's office at almost the same time as Fisher and his Sergeant. The latter carrying a large pseudo-paper folder. Ms Pearson greeted them with a smile, and directed them to another room. The only furniture was a large rectangular table with ten chairs set in two neat rows. Vice President Goldberg and Chief Superintendent Dixon were already seated. The four entered and took seats around the table. The Manager seated herself opposite Stone. "Your partner's not coming?" she enquired.

Stone sat forward, "She should be here by now, I guess she's held up. I apologise. Maybe we can begin with a brief summary from me on what we have achieved."

Pearson nodded, "As you please."

Stone outlined what they had uncovered during the investigation but omitted the deaths of the men at the mine. He described how the diamonds had found and how they had been shipped without manifest. Goldberg nodded a couple of times and formed his fingers into a steeple. Dixon looked very uncomfortable.

Stone also indicated that this was just a smuggling racket and that the shuttle disaster was simply a criminal activity that had gone badly wrong. He omitted their suspicions about possible political agendas and the apparent demise of Carlsen. Also he glossed over as fanciful, the existence of a dangerous organisation the Lunar Protection Society. That revelation raised disbelieving eye brows all around the table.

"But surely, that is precisely what you came here for, Mr Stone," said Goldberg with a smile, "Now that you have uncovered a smuggling racket and determined that there is no threat to the Base, then surely this investigation is over."

"Not quite," said Stone smiling. "There is a small matter of one of our agents, Eric Carlsen. We suspect he is not simply missing but is probably dead. Also there is the matter of sabotage. I refer to the second Shuttle accident and the reactor scram. There is no doubt about the second Shuttle being sabotaged, resulting in the death of the pilot. Or about the reactor being deliberately damaged. These questions need to be answered before I can close the enquiry."

Goldberg eased forward in his seat, "Do you have any theories regarding any of these incidents?"

"Yes, but they are just that, theories. When my partner arrives she may be able to shed some light on one of incidents. However, regarding the second Shuttle accident, I think that someone on the Base was worried that I or my partner had passed information to the pilot. After all, she did smuggle us onto the base, however unsuccessfully. The means of triggering that fatal accident was quite ingenious. I can discuss that now if your wish?"

Goldberg smiled, sitting back in his chair "I'm sure we will be fascinated."

"Well two things are required to start a launch sequence. The first requires the physical pressing of the Launch Activation Button, and the second requires an audible command given by the recognisable voiceprint of the pilot. Coming back to the second requirement, we now know that this was achieved with a recording being placed in the public address system. We cannot prove the first requirement, because we cannot talk to a vital witness who has just been murdered. However, a good guess would be that a maintenance worker pressed the button, before the pilot came on board. The worker then left the Shuttle and electronically activated the recording. I believe I know who that person was; but again, I cannot prove it."

Just then Susan entered, smiled at everyone around the table and winked at her husband.

"Welcome Mrs Stone," said Goldberg, "Your husband has just

finished briefing us on what has been uncovered. I have to say, I am appalled by what has been going on. Rest assured, heads will roll." He looked at Pearson, she, in turn, flinched.

Stone interjected. "Time for recrimination later, now let's hear from my partner."

Susan stood up and walked towards the electro-touch whiteboard.

Stopping with her back to the table and using just her finger on the board's surface, she wrote three names:

Eric Carlsen
Pauline Hicks
Mark Graham

Susan spoke as if she was lecturing a class of children, "Three names that all have something in common, they all died within the last five months. The first name is our agent who went missing. We now believe he's deceased. He was sent to assess the possibility of an organisation that had made threats against this Base. He filed a report but that report was incomplete. He disappeared at about the same time as the first Shuttle incident."

She pointed to the board. "The second name is the Captain from the second Shuttle incident. She was caught standing when someone deliberately activated a launch sequence while the Shuttle was being loaded onto the Launch-Rail. The question of why, currently remains unanswered. It does not make sense for smugglers to deliberately sabotage their only means of transport."

Stone coughed, "Er, I think I just covered that one."

"Ok…." She pressed her finger on the board and underlined the last name.

"The third name is that of a maintenance worker who we now think was responsible for the Reactor scram. I recently uncovered a missing pathology toxicology analysis from his autopsy report. It indicates that there was an extremely high level of potassium chloride in his system also within his stomach was a quantity of an unknown organophosphate. Potassium chloride, as you may or may not be aware, can cause heart failure in sufficient quantities. In fact, during the last century it was used in judicial executions. The problem with this substance is, that it is required to be injected. No puncture marks were found. Mark Graham, according to Ms Pearson, was drinking a cup of something when he died."

She turned to the Manager who said.

"Yes, that is what I thought, but I don't really know. I didn't actually see him drink. The personnel health monitor only activates in my office when the heart actually stops."

"I see. So the exact time of death or when his heart stopped is known, but nothing else. Is that correct?"

"Yes I suppose so, I didn't see the dead man on my screen until after the alarm went off, when I scanned his room. That is when I saw the cup lying on the floor near his hand."

"Is it true that you were instructed to play down an event such as this, days before the reactor incident?"

"Yes, I had been receiving instructions from someone on Earth to play down any unusual incidents. They threatened to hurt my mother if I did not cooperate."

"And why can you speak freely now?"

"I have evidence that my mother is now safe."

Both Goldberg and Dixon sat up, eyes wide.

Goldberg was out of his seat, "This is preposterous. Why would anyone want to do that? The woman is delusional, overworked and obviously needs a holiday."

The Manager was on her feet also, "I tell the truth …. I am not the only one that's been threatened."

Susan raised her hand, palm forward, "Settle down both of you. Mr Goldberg, our investigation service has uncovered a number of cases such as this. All of these people work in key positions on this Base, just accept it.

"Anyway, that's beside the point. Getting back to the Graham case, I cannot say if the cup contained poison, because the cup mysteriously disappeared. What I can say is, he was exposed to an organophosphate substance, probably odourless, colourless and tasteless and highly neurotoxic. I can say this because the man's cholinesterase level was down to less than 10% of normal. That indicates a massive exposure to an organophosphate neurotoxic agents or some other powerful cholinesterase inhibitor. To make it clear … cholinesterase is an enzyme that resets the nerve ending or neurones after they have been triggered by a chemical stimulus from the brain. For instance, a message comes from the brain to a muscle to contract, the muscle instructing it to contracts; the nerve is reset to neutral, if you like, by cholinesterase. If cholinesterase is destroyed or significantly inhibited, the nerves do not reset to a quiescent state, resulting in paralysis of the neural system.

"Note, it appears that whatever agent this was, it was exceedingly rapid in its action. There are only certain types of neurotoxic agents capable of such rapid action. One of these is a banned agent developed at the beginning of the Cold War in the last century. It also is odourless, tasteless and very rapid acting. This may not have killed him quickly enough for our murderer. So I presume, after he was unconscious someone injected a lethal dose of potassium salt. How this was done I'm not sure, but possibly an injection under the tongue."

Dixon stood up and was about to speak.

Susan raised her voice to a threatening level. "I suggest you remain seated, we have not finished yet." Dixon sat down.

Susan went back to the board, "I forgot, I need to add another name to this list."

She wrote:

Albert Copeland

That brought an immediate reaction from Goldberg, he looked as if he was about to faint. Susan turned to face her audience again.

"This last one," she paused, "died today. He died as a result of decompression in an airlock. There's a lot of that going around at the moment. I have just come from the Engineering section. The Chief Engineer, has examined the airlock door control unit, situated inside the lock itself. He reports that there are clear signs of tampering. The inner door lock interface circuit was completely disconnected. It would be impossible for anyone inside the airlock to open the inner door. Somebody, inside Armstrong must have cycled the outer airlock hatch."

By now there was absolute chaos in the room, everyone talking at once.

Just then the door swung open and Miles entered and Dixon jumped to his feet.

"Paul Miles! Where the hell have you been, the whole Service has been looking for you!"

Miles Smiled, "That's nice. Did you miss me Dixon? Oh by the way there is a Head of Section in Ottawa that wants a word with you … if you get my meaning?"

Miles took centre stage, "Thank you Susan, I think our guests have the picture." He moved to the head of the table and held up his hand to stem any questions.

"Now let me fill you in on the details. About two years ago diamonds in fairly large quantities were discovered in the Lunar deep mine. While this in itself is a most unlikely but hugely profitable event, the fact that they exist cannot be disputed. Whether the deposit was a result of ancient volcanic action or meteor impact is irrelevant. What is relevant is that their existence was kept a State secret. Countries that rely on these stones for revenue, naturally did not wish their products to be devalued by a sudden influx of reasonably cheap diamonds. TransGlobal agreed to limit extraction and release in return for lucrative Senate contracts. All worked well until the Senate elections, which are forecast for next year… and two candidates are neck and neck in the race.… Do you follow me Mr, Goldberg? Or Shall I go more slowly?"

Goldberg's face was almost purple and he was sweating profusely.

Miles continued, "We now have evidence that some people in the World Senate are getting a kickback in diamonds to alter the vote in favour of one of the candidates. The diamonds came from here in such huge quantities that the glut became obvious to the trade. Furthermore, these diamonds are very special in their mineral content and are easily identified. Investigation Branch challenged me to look into the situation, so the Lunar Protection Society was raised in status from a crackpot organisation to one posing a direct threat. Sorry, Stone," said Miles with a sickly smile.

"So I arranged for a threat message to be leaked to the Senate which then promptly issued an authority for us to investigate Armstrong Base.

"We did not anticipate what happened next. That was the sabotage to the reactor. It appears that after our bogus threat was issued, the real crackpot organisation took it upon itself to carry out an act of minor sabotage. They threatened poor old Mark Graham with exposure of his larcenous past that would result in him losing his job. They said that all he had to do was disable the reactor for a brief period. This he did. However, the act drew attention to Armstrong's other activities causing an investigator to be sent to the Base. Graham was disposed of because he was a threat. His actions had brought the Base onto CIS' radar and that could not be tolerated. Therefore Graham had to go. As a precaution, someone organised the kidnap of the families of people in various key positions, then set up a system to secretly ship diamonds under the cover of legitimate cargoes."

Miles paused a moment to gauge the effect of his revelations. "You may think this is an awful lot of trouble to go to." Miles picked up the bag he had been carrying and tipped its contents onto the table. "Let me assure you, that what you are looking at, plus the other two bags that I have in my possession, are the equivalent of the entire Gross National Product of the North American continent." He picked a handful of stones and let them dribble dramatically through his fingers.

"The next incidents that prompted further investigation by me, was the first Shuttle disaster and subsequent loss of my agent. The first Shuttle incident, as has been explained, was a combination of bad programming and stupidity. The second incident was to remove my other agent whome I would now like to introduce, Come in Dear." All heads turned, and standing before them like a ghost was Pauline Hicks, the Shuttle Captain.

"Come in Pauline, take a seat."

She sat. "Hi everyone" She looked at Stone and winked "Sorry to scare you, Honey."

Miles continued, "Pauline was injured but not too seriously, so she immediately co-opted the help of the treating physician to give her assistance. Because she was worried that her life was in danger. Pauline reported to me about the sabotage to her Shuttle. I wasn't sure if this was another crackbrain scheme by the real LPS, or something else. So not wishing to lose another Agent I directed Pauline to take the Doctor further into her confidence and for him to arrange her premature demise. How, is the Doctor by the way?"

"Very cute, very shy and he's terribly worried about the ethics relating to patient / doctor relationships." She shrugged and smiled lasciviously.

Stone laughed out loud. Susan looked from her husband to the Pilot, with a suspicious expression on her face.

Miles turned to Stone, "Sorry Harry, it was Pauline that removed the data from your computer, the whole scheme was coming apart. After you were drugged by none other than Albert Copeland, Pauline called me that you were acting in a strange manner. So, after you fell asleep, she skin tested you for drugs and guess what she detected psychotrone our own product. Acting under my instructions, she disabled your computer and removed the printout. We could not afford for you to retain any data, until you were cleared by Springfield. So I arranged a call to you to get you into the pilot's cabin and to arrange for you to stay at Gamma 5. It was then that the rogue agents acted. They could not afford to kill me, my profile is too high so the next best thing was to have me committed

Stone remembered sitting next to Copeland in the canteen, before the flight.

"Anyway, that's the story up to now, except for one thing. Who is benefitting from the diamond sales? Well, I can answer that also….. You, Mr Goldberg, and your partners in crime."

Goldberg stood up shouting at Miles, he was completely incoherent.

"And you Mr Dixon and your rogue Agents are accomplices in crime for profit. It is surprising what large quantities of money can buy. How much is he paying you?" Dixon looked at his feet.

Ah! There is one other ….." Miles did not get to finish his sentence before Fisher was on his feet with his Sergeant. Both had small handguns. Pearson was on her feet also shouting. "Don't be stupid, there is nowhere you can go, and those weapons will pierce the station wall and kill all of us."

Fisher smiled at the Manager, "These weapons contain frangible bullets that is, they break apart if they hit anything solid. They're the type used by security guards on military airfields. However they have no problem penetrating the soft human body, unless they hit bone, of course. In which case they will fragment with lethal force into the body." He smiled and pointed the gun at the Manager "I always said I would get my own back on you. Now is my chance. I have nothing to lose." He turned to Miles and re-aimed the weapon, "How did you know?"

Miles put up his hands as he spoke, "Not hard really, once we had all the facts. It was Stone who became suspicious when he and Susan were attacked that first time. Who else but you knew what they had discovered and where they were going? That in itself was not enough until they were attacked a second time in the deep mine. Again who knew what was planned? Only you. As far as the Mine manager was concerned they were simply investigating a missing person. The last issue clinched it. You killed Albert Copeland to prevent him from talking to Stone and revealing that he had loaded Eric Carlsen on the Shuttle, adjusted the load manifest and fixed the Launch Computer so that any load discrepancies would not prevent the launch. That was your big mistake. Only Stone, Susan, the Load Controller, and of course … you, knew that Stone was closing in on Copeland. You could not afford that, so he died. After that, it was logical that you'd probably had Mark Graham killed as well. That one was particularly nasty. Graham by his action had brought your operation onto the CIS radar, so you decided to kill him and give yourself an alibi. You put a nerve agent into Graham's water, and when he drank it, he became unconscious very quickly. Then you injected Graham with the potassium salt. He was a dead man from that point. When Rosemary called you to inform you of his death, you reacted as she would have expected you to. Then, acting as a concerned police officer, you went to Graham's room and removed the cup. You even very carefully washed the man's mouth and hands with soap and water, to remove as much of the neurotoxin as possible. You sealed the room while your sergeant here arranged a thorough clean-up. Then you contacted your 'masters' Earth-side who instructed Ms Pearson to cover up the death, to arranged for the post mortem results to be lost and to move the Doctor to where he could not be contacted. Close enough? I have to say your act as an outraged Security Officer was very convincing. You had everyone fooled … for a while at least."

"Very clever Mr. Miles." Fisher extended his arm and aimed the gun at Miles' head, "You first I think."

There was a sudden blur of movement from both ends of the room. Pauline struck Fisher's gun to one side and at same time, rammed the side of her stiffened hand into his windpipe. Fisher crumpled to the ground, gasping to draw air through his ruined larynx. Susan had caught the Sergeant by surprise and promptly twisted his head around 'til his neck snapped with a grating crunch. His body twisted and he slowly collapsed to the ground and lay there unmoving. Both Goldberg and Dixon were frozen into immobility, each with an expression of incredulous horror on his.

Miles looked mildly shocked, "Wow that was a bit exciting. I'm glad I'm not a Field Agent."

Stone stood up and walked over to Fisher, who was still gasping for breath and muttered "Bastard, Bastard! …" He then turned to Springfield. "Max and his boys are outside; get them in here to take care of these four beauties.

The Manager Rosemary was quietly sobbing in one corner of the room.

Springfield opened the door, Max was waiting outside. "I don't suppose you heard any of that." Max laughed, "Hard not to when you hold a glass to the door." He sheepishly held up a long stemmed drinking glass, "Excellent stethoscope." Springfield laughed, Then I suppose I can leave you to clean this up?" "My pleasure, mate," said Max holding up a handful of cable ties.

Fisher was taken to the Medical Centre under close guard of Max's engineers. He would probably never talk clearly again without a prosthetic larynx.

Springfield, Miles and Captain Hicks decided to head for the bar. "What about your new friend the Doctor?" said Springfield. Pauline gave a sly smile, "I guess he will join us after he finished fixing that bastard Fisher. Strange, I didn't think I hit him that hard, he must have a glass jaw." They walked out laughing.

Left alone, Susan and Stone looked at each other. Then as only long term lovers can, read each other's thoughts. "Home, lady-killer, said Stone" Susan put her arms round his waist and drew him in tight, and was about to kiss him when a voice sounded behind them. "Hemm!" Rosemary Pearson was smiling at them, "I don't want to spoil anyone's fun. But what about these." She pointed to the gems on the table. "Damn. I guess I can put them in the safe in Security with the rest." He scooped up the stones and put them into the bag. I'll see you at home, Honey, as soon as I've locked this lot up. They've caused enough bother to last two lifetimes." Stone picked up the bag and headed for the Security Section where the duty officer was sitting behind Fisher's old desk, drinking one of Fisher's special drinks.

He stood up as Stone entered. "Carry on," said Stone, I don't think the owner will mind." The duty officer looked sheepish. "I hear he may be away for a very long time. Oh, I'm Maurice Hurst, the new Head of Security."

"Well Maurice, Where can I secure this lot?" said Stone, opening the bag.

"Bloody hell, where did that lot come from?"

"Never mind, where can I secure it?"

Maurice walked over to a wall panel and pressed six digits onto the keypad, and what appeared to be part of the wall swung outward, revealing a very sturdy looking metal door with an electronic combination lock on the front. "In there. I think they should be safe. Key in your own combination code, then that will be the only way to open it." The door was already slightly open. The instructions on the front told to press the #* signs together, enter any combination letters and numbers, then press * again. Stone keyed in his combination and the door lock clicked. Stone placed the sack into the safe and closed the door, the mechanism whined and clicked again.

Stone was just tuning to thank Maurice when the door slammed open and Fisher appeared. He had blood soaking the front of his jumpsuit and a blood-spattered fire axe in his hand.

"Where are they?" he wheezed, his voice barely audible. "The diamonds, where are they?"

As Stone backed away from the door Maurice reached for the alarm switch. There was a blur of shiny steel and he fell to the floor, leaving his hand on the desk, he grasped at the stump of his arm as the axe started to swing again.

Stone stepped forward and shouted, "No!" the axe paused in half swing. "If you want you're the diamonds then I'll give them to you, but leave him alone."

Fisher lowered the axe, "Where are they?" he croaked.

"In the safe, and I have the combination. Kill me and you lose."

"Bugger you!" shouted Fisher raising the axe again and aiming it at his victim.

"Then I won't kill you, I'll kill him!"

"Ok, Fisher, you win" shouted Stone, "You win."

"Open the safe now!" repeated Fisher.

Stone knew that the moment he opened the safe he was a dead man. His mind was whirling. This really wasn't his trade. Unlike Susan and Springfield he was an analyst. The thought of Springfield reminded him of the thing under the skin of his forearm. He had been conscious of it as an ever present lump, ever since Springfield put it there. What did he say? — Press the lump very hard with a fingernail remember, very hard! All this went through his head while he was fiddling with the safe's door. He still hadn't decided what to do, when Fisher laid the blade of the axe on the side of his neck.

He jumped away from the safe, Fisher stalking him. "Oh, well, what the ...." He reached across with his right hand and found the lump. Taking a deep breath he pressed the lump with his thumbnail ... nothing! Fisher was swaying towards him swinging the axe, a look of pure hate on his face. Stone pressed the lump again ... still nothing. He was watching Fisher and was almost mesmerised by the swinging blade. Whatever was supposed to have happened should have done so by now, he thought. Then he remembered the bit about "Real Hard." He pressed the lump again with his thumbnail, this time using all his strength. He felt something pop inside his arm and a warm glow spread from the spot where the lump had been. Then colours altered, as everything about him slowed. Fisher said something, but it was so low and slow that he could not understand what he had said. The swinging blade had almost slowed to a stop. He move towards Fisher, but misjudged the distance and crashed into him. Stone reached for the axe and easily took it from Fisher's grasp. He threw the axe away, not seeing where it went. Fisher was almost standing still. Stone thought about all the men that this man had controlled or killed, and rage went through him. He swung his fist at Fisher's nose. The nose collapsed and the bones from the nose powdered with fragments driving deep into Fisher's face. Then Stone, simply wanting to slap Fisher's face, missed and hit the side of the man's head instead. The head moved to the left and there was a very low-pitched crunching noise. Fisher, appeared to slowly collapse onto the floor, his head at a very unnatural angle.

Stone sat on the floor next to the injured Security Officer, looked up and saw the axe buried deep in the wall smiled, and immediately fell asleep, and snoring loudly.

Stone slowly clawed his way back to consciousness. The first thing he noticed was a bright light shining in his eyes. It moved from side to side. A voice, a quite pleasant and familiar voice was talking but not making any sense. Then he heard Susan's voice He opened his eyes but everything was blurry. Gradually his eyes focused, and there was the Doctor and Susan standing next to him, both looking down at him. Then he distinctly heard Susan say. "He's awake." But her voice was oddly deep. The Doctor replied, "He needs to stay on the protein glucose drip for the rest of the day, and then some." Painfully slowly Susan kissed him on the forehead and said, "Welcome back Darling."

He didn't understand — where had he been? Then he went to sleep again.

He dreamt of Singapore and his family, sitting with him on a beach under a warm tropical sun. His son was playing on the sand and he was sipping a very cold martini. He felt a sting in his right arm as though a mosquito had bitten him. Then for no reason he was cold and tried to get up from the sand, but a firm hand pressed him back and suddenly he was wide awake. This time everything was normal. He knew where he was. Susan was sitting by the bed with Miles and Springfield. The Doctor was checking his blood pressure and scanning his body functions with his Med Scanner.

The doctor smiled, "All good, he's back."

"Susan leaned over him and kissed his lips hard. That more than anything brought him rapidly back to reality. Miles had a slightly worried look on his face, which was unusual because it was firmly believed in the Service that Miles was incapable of any emotion.

"Welcome back son. We've been worried about you."

Springfield smiled. "I guess you were in real trouble."

Stone's throat was dry and he had trouble speaking. "How long have I been asleep?"

The doctor answered, "Six days, not including our first resuscitation attempt."

"What the hell happened? The last thing I remember was Fisher swinging an axe at the new Security Officer. After that there are just snatches of memory about pressing something on my arm?"

"I guess I'm responsible," said Miles. "I instructed Springfield to issue you the new drug capsule that had been developed to enhance perceptual and real-time speed. The trouble with the drug is, it forces your body to consume its nourishment resources at 2.5 times the normal rate. In twenty seconds you used up half of your glucose and a third of your fat reserves. The drug acts by stimulating mitochondria to produce a huge surge of energy in all the cells of your body. The drug is still not on general issue because most of the agents that have actually used it died of malnutrition and exhaustion after about three days. You are actually the first to survive."

Susan looked at Miles with a very dangerous look on her face.

"Anyway," continued Miles, "If we hadn't given you the capsule, you'd have likely been dead anyway. The Officer we interviewed says that Fisher was crazy." Miles leaned away from Susan and smiled, "The Security Officer, who is recovering well in Montreal Hospital, gave us a full brief on what he saw. He has now been retired from the Company Security Service and will be working for us in the Ottawa office. We can't have that kind of information floating about uncontrolled."

Stone remembered a brief picture of Fisher falling to the ground in slow motion. "What happened to Fisher?"

"You don't remember?" "You sort of slapped his head so hard that three vertebrae were crushed and his spinal cord was ripped in two places."

Suddenly Stone felt very weary ... "I think I need to sleep…"

EPILOGUE

The Earth Shuttle landed at Nassau Landing Field. Miles and Springfield descended the stairs leading from the Shuttle, followed by Stone, Susan and Pauline. They had remained at Armstrong for a further four weeks tying up loose ends and making sure that the people who were being reunited with their families got away safely. There had been a complete turnover of the management personnel, and new systems had been put in place to monitor the shipping of cargoes. Sadly, Max would not be part of the new organisation. He had been killed during Fisher's escape bid. Stone was still very weak from his brush with the drug that pharmacologists had aptly named *Lightning*. He had lost twenty kilos in three weeks, and was only now starting to put weight back on. Susan said that they should water down the product and patent it as a weight reduction drug.

Stepping into the bright sunlight, Miles spread his arms wide and sighed, "Oh, it's so good to be back!"

Springfield touched his arm, "We still have the big job to do before we can rest, boss. Do you have any idea who in the Service is behind all this, it can't just be Dixon on his own?"

"As a matter of fact, I do," Miles replied.

"Who?"

"Wait and see or ask Stone, he's probably worked it out by now. Oh, by the way, I'm having you transferred to my Department and we are going after the rotten agents in CIS."

"That's encouraging." said Springfield, cautiously rolling his eyes upward.

Stone finally caught up with the two as they entered the terminal building. "What now, Paul?

Miles looked at Stone, "I think I will leave this one to you grasshopper. You can take care of the CEO TransGlobal and his partners, and I will take care of the CIS. You know what to do. Now, I'm going to my hotel to take a very long shower. See you when you get back to Singapore." Miles turned and walked briskly to the Customs clearance area.

Springfield shrugged and smiled weakly at Stone, "I guess we have some interesting times ahead of us. Take care, my friend. Be careful. With Paul Miles you never know where we will end up, but I have a feeling that we will be working together again real soon." With that he shook hands with Stone and gave Susan a hug and was gone.

Susan and Stone cleared Customs and Quarantine and headed for the booking desk. "So Miles wants us to clean up TransGlobal in Geneva while he cleans up the CIS side of things in Montreal. Either way, Honey, there are going to be many vacancies in both organisations over the next few months. Our brief is to root out those that were involved with the Senate bribery scam." Stone looked thoughtfully at his wife. "You know, if the CEO of TransGlobal had become president our lives wouldn't be worth much right now. I do feel sorry in a bent sort of way for poor Goldberg. He took all the risks, and if his boss had become President then he would have been the next CEO. That was his real prize in all of this. Now the CEO is already in custody and it appears that twenty-two Senate seats are up for grabs, and climbing."

Susan looked unhappy and pouted, and cut across his reverie, "Do we have to leave today? I'd love to spend a couple of days in Nassau, on the beach, please, Honey."

Stone thought about it for only a moment, Susan's idea of the beach was very inviting, but he could hear Paul Miles berating him for delay … No, Susan was far more dangerous than Miles, "Ok, Honey but only two days in Nassau, agreed? Remember that if our Chief Inspector becomes President, guess who may be promoted into his job. Do we really want to be around when that happens?"

"Then maybe we should take a long holiday in Singapore after we get back from Geneva?" He smiled contentedly, as she threw herself round his neck.

Canggu Bali 1 September 2016

AUTHOR'S NOTES

Magnetic Linear Accelerators exist now. They have been trialled by the US Navy to launch aircraft from carriers. Also magnetic levitation railways are operational today. All that I have done is scale the system up to launch Space craft. Of course launching from the moon has advantages due to the sparsity of its atmosphere, (near vacuum) reducing friction.

Helium three is an integral component of Fusion Reactors. On Earth He3 is very rare and the main source of supply at the moment is China which holds most the world's stock. While He3 is rare on Earth, it is found in plentiful supply within the lunar soil.

Is it possible that diamonds could be found on the moon? The answer is, nobody can be certain one way or the other. Certainly the moon did have a volcanic past, some 3-4 Billion years ago, and if, as it has been suggested, the moon did calve from the Earth during the creation of the planets, it is possible that some of the elements making up the crust of the moon may be similar to those found on Earth. Despite all of this, astronomers have discovered a planet in a nearby star system that is made almost entirely of diamond and some solar bodies such as meteors and asteroids do contain high levels of carbon or even diamond. Just perhaps, a collision with of one of these produced the necessary heat and pressure to create diamonds in our story.

With regards to the human body being exposed to a vacuum — sorry, they don't explode nor do their eyes don't pop out. A NASA engineer testing a space suit was accidentally exposed to a vacuum for 15 seconds and he lived. The thing he said he remembered most was the saliva boiling off his tongue. The human body is like a sack and is sufficiently strong to keep the organs inside even at an internal pressure of 14 pounds per square inch. It is inevitable that a person exposed long term to a vacuum would die of asphyxiation, but he would not freeze because his body heat could not transfer through the vacuum. He might suffer the bends as the gases in his blood bubbled out of solution. If an attempt was made to hold ones breath, it is possible that the lungs would rupture. There might be petechial spots on the surface of the skin as small blood vessels rupture, and possibly the soft tissue of the eyes might bleed. As for the dramatic exploding deaths as depicted in some movies, sorry, that has not been demonstrated in any experiments so far conducted,